WEREWOLF
WC
COUNCIL

# NOBILITATE NOBIS

## J. MANOA

**E**

**EPIC**
Escape

An Imprint of EPIC Press
EPICPRESS.COM

# Nobilitate Nobis
## Werewolf Council: Book #3

Written by J. Manoa

Published by EPIC Press™
PO Box 398166
Minneapolis, MN 55439

Cover design by Candice Keimig & Neil Klinepier
Images for cover art obtained from iStockPhoto.com
Edited by Ryan Hume

LIBRARY OF CONGRESS CATALOGING-IN-PUBLICATION DATA
Names: Manoa, J., author.
Title: Nobilitate nobis / by J. Manoa.
Description: Minneapolis, MN : EPIC Press, 2018. | Series: Werewolf council ; #3
Summary: A series of killings threatens to shred the secret peace between the werewolves and
    guardians of Stumpvale. Both Nate and Riley become unwilling centers of attention on their
    respective sides until finally, the peace unravels, and everything changes.
Identifiers: LCCN 2016946215 | ISBN 9781680765007 (lib. bdg.)
    | ISBN 9781680765564 (ebook)
Subjects: LCSH: Friendship—Fiction. | Murder—Fiction. | Werewolves—Fiction. | Young
    adult fiction.
Classification: DDC [Fic]—dc23
LC record available at http://lccn.loc.gov/2016946215

EPIC
Press

EPICPRESS.COM

*For Nick and Alenka*

# PROLOGUE

"**W**HERE THE HELL ARE WE, AGAIN?"

"Stumpvale."

"The hell kinda name is that?"

Michael Murray leaned from the camera to shrug. He straightened up, closed one eye, and stared into the side lens. His uncovered ear lightly brushed the compartment that held the videotape along with a digital recording device. Everything he shot would be kept on file in case there was ever a need to reference the story again later. Or in case another bird flew into Rebecca's hair and caused her to scream and run off while shouting a string of profanities that would have gotten the network fined if they weren't airing live.

"How's the makeup?" Rebecca Egbe asked, looking into the camera in front of her.

Murray gave a thumbs-up with one hand while the other adjusted the focus on the long lens. He inched one foot forward into the gap between the legs of the tripod.

"I don't want to look too shiny in the light out here." Egbe reached into the pocket of her windbreaker. Checking herself again in the mirror of her compact, she smoothed down a flake of makeup at the top of her nostril. Murray zoomed in on the back of her hands, the long fingernails that Rebecca spent nearly the entire drive from Juneau covering in countless layers of polish. The smell had made him so woozy that he'd been afraid he'd crash into a tree.

She put the compact down and immediately went out of focus. He adjusted the lens once more to bring her face into the shot. The fountain at the center of the plaza, the paths branching out in three directions, and the trees off the paths gave a nice frame he was sure no one would appreciate.

"Is this going live?"

"Well," Murray replied, "almost live."

"Dammit, you screw up once and they punish you forever. It was the bird's damn fault."

"One minute till air," Murray said, echoing the voice over his headset.

"One minute, seven seconds," Rebecca commented.

"Hey, station got complaints. A lot of them."

"Yeah, and all the YouTube comments were that the bird mistook my hair for its nest," she said, muttering, "when they weren't yakking about my chest." She took that moment to pull the zipper on her windbreaker down just a little more. She patted the top of her hair.

"How is it?" she asked.

"Not at all nest-like."

The camera clearly showed her roll her eyes and give it the finger.

"Thirty seconds until live."

"One slip and I go from covering the State of the State, to tabloid stories in Podunk logging towns."

Murray tried not to laugh as he added another item to the list of videos he'd copy if he ever decided to quit. "Ten seconds," he said.

Egbe breathed in and out slowly, glancing down to make sure that the mic was clipped high enough on her collar that it didn't distract from the line of cleavage.

"Five, four, three," Murray gestured the final two numbers.

"Good evening, Jack. The small community here in Stumpvale was shocked last night at the discovery of an entire family found dead in their home. Police tells us that the incident took place early Thursday morning in the residence of Roderick and Melanie Bailey, who lived there with their two sons, Liam and Connor. Details are sketchy as of right now, but witnesses are saying that the scene included words written in blood on the wall. The bodies were allegedly piled in the living room. While no identifying marks have been found, several long and very thick white hairs have reportedly been picked up from near the bodies. The incident took place just over twenty-four hours after Liam Bailey's girlfriend, eighteen-year-old Dawn Musgrave, was found dead on the railroad tracks outside of the town. Liam Bailey had reported the crime to the police and was believed to be the only witness. Both incidents are currently being investigated, but so far no arrests have been made. Meanwhile, the town's residents are baffled, frightened, and wondering what will happen next."

"Forty seconds back," Murray said as the studio cut to a package they'd made earlier that day, asking residents for their thoughts on the "recent string of murders."

"Already sick of that word," Egbe remarked. "Incident. Everything is a damn incident. Call it what it is."

Murray leaned away to shrug again.

"Saying 'murder' might cause panic," she said in a mocking tone. "The national networks are nothing but twenty-four-hour panic."

"Ten seconds back."

Egbe gathered herself as Murray counted down.

"These are the first major crimes in Stumpvale since a similar event twenty years ago, when another family was found dead in their home, and a fourth victim was later located in the woods. The murderer in that case remained at large for three years before being tracked to a cabin ten miles outside of the town. For now, local officials recommend caution, but believe that modern technology and greater community cooperation will bring this case to a swift end. Back to you, Jack . . ."

"And we're out," Murray said, yanking the headset off from his backwards cap. He started dismantling the tripod.

"How was that?" Egbe asked, unclipping the mic from her collar before zipping her windbreaker all the way up.

"Fine," Murray replied, pulling the camera off the stand. "But you overused the word 'incident.'"

He didn't look as she rolled her eyes again.

"All right, think there's a place I can get a decent meal in this town, or it is all gonna be moose meat and shrew steaks?"

Murray shook his head, wishing he'd left the camera running just a little longer.

On one of the benches where the path curved behind them, a man in a long coat held his gloved hands in his lap. He kept his eyes closed in concentration, listening as the reporter continued to say that at least she wasn't sent to one of those tiny places with only a couple hundred people who insist that their stories are just as important as those that happen in the real cities. The man rubbed at the sleeve of his long coat. He looked at his arm. Focusing, he sensed the scratches in the flesh beneath. The names of Roderick, Melanie, Connor, and Liam Bailey, along with Dawn Musgrave, were all but faded from his forearm. Above them, several more faintly visible scars led up the length of his inner arm.

The first name, faded long ago from the curve beneath his shoulder, was Patrick Wallace. He'd have to pay for each of them someday.

He closed his eyes, rubbed his gloved hands together, and concentrated on listening to the reporter and the cameraman packing up their gear.

That day couldn't come soon enough.

# CHAPTER 1

**S**HE COULD HEAR THAT SAME, MOCKING GIGGLE. It sounded like a little girl eager to begin a game. Like whatever Riley did, she'd never be more than a fun playmate.

Riley pressed her teeth together and felt the pressure all the way up her jaw. She felt it more than in her feet, calves, knees, thigh, hips, or any other place that she expected to ache after a series of quick lunges and tumbles. Instead, there was almost nothing. She felt the air over her fingers more than the movement of muscles under skin.

Dove landed in a wide crouch, one knee bent

and the other straight, one hand on the ground. Her gaze followed Riley upward, her hood shadowing her face with a dense darkness. Dove giggled again. Riley growled at this. She flicked her wrist, the wooden sword in her hand giving the tiniest tug on her forearm. Dove had already taken the low stance—only one place to go from there. Riley gripped her blade's hilt in both hands and positioned the sword across herself. She slid her left foot back easily, as though there were no weight on it at all, and stared into the void between Dove's hood and the cloth over her nose and mouth, the only shadow Riley couldn't see through. Dove would see the same shadow under Riley's own hood.

Riley picked up the vibration in Dove's cloak. The hood lifted very slightly as she started to move, and Riley was off the ground before Dove could strike. The jump was nothing. Riley tucked her legs to avoid her pouncing opponent, and inertia spun her into a frontflip. She angled the sword upward. The edge of the wooden blade caught the tail of

Dove's cloak. She watched dust particles flutter from the friction between wood and cloth. Riley spun on her toes as she landed in a pirouette on the stone floor. There was a tug at the side of her cloak. The hood pulled against her forehead. Dove swept around to watch her, one hand on the ground again. The sword in her other hand pointed back toward the circular wall of the room, the few other recruits who stood as witness to their session. Riley stared ahead at Dove, waiting to see the air move. Dove lowered her stance. Riley's hood lifted and then dropped into the top of her vision. She kept the sword in one hand and yanked the hood back with the other.

"Stop!"

Dove rose from her stance. Riley turned toward the sound. Virgil leaned against the stones lining the doorway into the main chamber. Every fold in his shirt was clear—every wrinkle on his face, as well.

"You're exposed," he said.

Riley yanked the cloth from across her face,

unbuttoning it from inside the hood. "It was restricting my movement," she replied. "She could already see me."

"She could, but the wolf will not unless you allow it to." The cracks and lines in the stones behind him stood out as the darkest of the innumerable gray hues.

"She's not a wolf."

"We don't practice to fight each other," Virgil said. His shirt shone in waves as he approached. "We practice to fight the wolf. Right now, your scent is loose. You're exposed." He placed one empty palm back as he stepped up to Riley. Dove slid her sword into Virgil's hand. "At this point," he said, "you've lost."

Riley exhaled hard through her nose. She straightened up, letting her sword drop toward the floor. The stones were shiny from years of footsteps, which had smoothed away the rough edges into slick surfaces.

"That's enough for now," Virgil said, glancing

back to Dove. The woman nodded, spun on her heels, and walked away. Her footsteps were light taps on the floor, a thin vibration in every other step. "Riley," Virgil said, coming to a stop a few feet in front of her, Dove's sword hanging from one loose arm, "we're done for today. You can drop it."

Riley blinked several times until the room faded into dim candlelight. The stones were a uniform gray, Virgil's shirt was a monotone white, his face was folds and shadow. He put his empty hand out, palm up. She handed him the sword.

"Three days and you're evading Dove's simplest strikes," he said with a nod. "You're on your way to becoming what you're meant to be."

"Thank you," she said.

"I'll summon Sister Kennera to take you back."

Riley nodded. She pulled at her hair band and shook her hair loose. The blond streak had grown out.

"Brother Julius, Brother Gregory," Virgil said,

turning toward two of the men lining the wall of the room. "The floor is yours."

Riley waited until she was out of the room before undoing the buttons and strings tying her cloak together. She turned left outside of the door, away from the paths to the office and the room where Virgil had given her the cup that healed her leg and gave her the strength to fight a corruption no one else could. Not that she had actually seen "the corruption" herself, not with her own eyes, not without doubt. She reached for the handle to the third door on the left, the same plain door with the same plain knob as all the others.

The barrack was organized into twelve individual bunks, pairs situated next to each other with enough room to walk between. Each living space had a bed with the foot facing the door; a wooden desk against the wall, with three wide drawers for clothes and one smaller top drawer for a Bible; a wooden chair; and a set of hooks on the wall next to the desk. Dove had already hung her cloak across three hooks, the arms spread to air out any residual scents prior to treatment. With all the cloaks hung in the same fashion, it gave the appearance of a dozen cloth crosses lining the barrack's walls. Dove genuflected in front of the garment, her cleanly shaved head angled down in reflection.

Riley tried to keep from staring as she approached her place in the room, second on the right. She removed her cloak to hang it, as well. She glanced at the clothes folded on the desk next to her. Three pieces of plastic cast were on the chair. The chair was meant for reading or sitting in quiet thought under the light of a sconce overhead. Her crutches leaned against it. They were purely cosmetic now.

Motion caught Riley's eye as she turned away from the hanging cloak. Dove sat down to remove the thin training shoes from her feet. One foot ended in a rounded metal point, like the bottom of Riley's crutches with the plastic cover removed. Riley shifted to kneeling at the bottom of the cloak.

She glanced quickly as Dove stood to undress. Dove's back was a topographical map. The dim lights turned every bone and muscle into a lighted peak or shaded valley. Her shoulder blades were mountains, her ribs were hills, her spine a fault through the middle. She had no scars or stray marks at all. Clean as a child. Riley bowed her head once more.

This was when she was supposed to pray, in the sight of one of the sacred symbols of the Order of the Hidden Blade. This was when she was supposed to ask God for the strength to deliver this world and its inhabitants from evil. She was supposed to thank Him for the offering which allowed her to be the light in the darkness and the shepherd for the sheep. She glanced up once more at the sound of fabric sliding. On Dove's left thigh, a wooden cuff started just below where her fingers could reach.

Riley quickly looked away again, whispering nonsense to herself in the place of a prayer. She felt the weight on her leg. A few days ago, she wouldn't have been able to kneel like this. She hadn't been able to walk. She had barely been able to sit for five minutes unless she kept her weight on the other side. The sound of Dove's footsteps caused her to look up again.

Dove's cuff ended at a metal hinge in the middle of her leg. The leg below the hinge rounded into a metal rod an inch in diameter. From the knee down, the leg looked like something from a campy pirate adventure, or the aftermath of a Civil War epic. It was a brutish contrast to the cast that Riley still pretended to need, held together by metal bolts in flesh instead of plastic and Velcro. Half of Dove's footsteps were hollow and metallic as she moved toward the washroom at the rear of the barrack. Each impact echoed through the artificial leg. Riley muttered "amen" before standing. She leaned all her weight to the side she hadn't been able to use for weeks. She felt nothing.

Riley glanced around the room. Cloaks had been removed from the bunks for Sisters Kennera and

Sarah. No one else was around. She undressed as well.

She slipped on the sweatpants with one side cut off. She paused after pulling her shirt down. Her arm was spotted with craters from shielding herself against flying glass. It had taken only a day for her bones to heal completely, yet the scars along the inside of her forearm marked every place the glass had entered. The scars on her face remained as well. That was one of the limitations of their "gift": it couldn't regrow limbs, vital organs probably wouldn't heal fast enough to prevent death, and anything that had healed before—ugly as it may be—was left as it was.

"You keep the old ones with you," Virgil had said following her first sacrament. "They are the sins of your previous life, before you were reborn in service of the Order." She remembered thinking then of the deep line on her father's chin. "Those you receive now, through His holy pursuit, are allowed to wash away." She also remembered rolling her eyes at Virgil's speech until she put her foot down.

It was her first unsupported step since the accident. There had been no pain since. Not in her leg.

# CHAPTER 2

**F**ROM WHERE NATE SAT, THE REPORTER WAS NO longer visible through the crowd, which stood in a half circle around him in the center of the plaza. Nate leaned forward on the bench, elbows on his knees, trying to hear anything that the reporter was saying but he was too far away, the sound too muffled by the throng of people surrounding him. If Nate weren't stuck here, on the bench and in this form, he would know everything that was being said. He'd even know how the crowd felt—if their adrenaline was peaking, or if they were sweating, and if it was a cooling sweat or a nervous one.

He could see a couple of folks attempting to slide from the end of the half circle to get a better view, but they were immediately waved back by a man wearing a baseball cap and carrying a small phone in his hand. The fountain a few feet behind the reporter kept people from gathering or approaching on the other side. This was the second reporter to come to the town in as many days.

"Can you hear him?" Nate asked, glancing to where Shayera sat slightly slouched on the opposite end of bench, one hand hanging limply off the armrest and one foot planted onto the seat in front of her.

"Not a word," she said. "Probably nothing solid."

"Doesn't matter," Nate replied, straightening against the seatback. "The speculation could be enough. The idea that something weird is happening will promote interest in the story."

Shayera looked at him quickly before returning to view the crowd. "Not the first time that's happened."

"Maybe, but like Maier said, the world is different now. Once a story gets out in one place, it's out everywhere. If a story is everywhere it must be true because everyone is talking about it. Trying to deny or disprove it just means you're trying to hide the truth." Nate recalled the comments on the conspiracy videos he'd seen online about Illuminati messages and how Stanley Kubrick faked the moon landing. Nate peeked toward Shayera. She didn't react. "There are werewolves in this town," he said, "and they're killing people."

She narrowed her eyes at this.

"Everyone's talking about it."

Shayera sighed heavily, lowering her head. "What do you suggest then?" She looked at him through the corners of her eyes. "That we listen to Maier? Out ourselves and hope humans don't hunt us down, even worse than they have before?"

Nate shook his head.

"Or maybe we should offer up one of our kind as the killer. A scapegoat. Who should we choose for that honor?" she said, a sharpness to her tone. "Knowing that whoever goes will be put on trial and then probably dissected in a lab. Would you want to do that?"

Nate shifted his view down and away.

"I wouldn't, and I wouldn't want you to do that either. I wouldn't wish that on any of us. Not even on Maier."

"Better it happen to one than to all," Nate replied, looking to the crowd just as it started to disperse. The news report must be over.

"No reason to worry," Shayera said, brushing her hands of the topic. "Threats like this happen all the time. Not exactly like this, but exposure is a danger anywhere we live. That's why we built little towns, so we can keep things quiet. The Council will deal with it. Ulrich has done it before."

Nate turned to see Shayera staring at him.

"Did a good job cleaning up after you," she said snidely.

There had been a doctor and a police officer near Nate's bed when he woke up in the hospital after the crash. One of them mentioned the Council. He couldn't remember which it was that said it, probably the cop, since he'd said that any evidence was lost or destroyed. His mother had been the first to mention a fire. People always use fire to get rid of evidence. Heat did that. Hell, tons of movies did that. Would the Council do it? Would Ulrich?

"Anyway," Shayera said, gesturing toward the crowd wandering away, "once the audience gets bored, the whole story will be forgotten."

"Assuming nothing new happens."

"It won't," Shayera said, nodding confidently. "We'll make sure of that."

Nate looked to where the reporter was speaking with the man in the hat as the cameraman packed up his gear. Former members of the crowd went back about their business, sitting on the benches, taking pictures in front of the fountain. One couple even retreated to the edges of the concrete before video-recording the reporter and the crew as they left. A couple of guys, Sam and Matt, walked the path toward Pine. They'd been in Nate's last two math classes. They'd hung out a couple of times along with Craig and Tony, and Riley, once. The two of them looked from Nate to Shayera, Matt lagged behind to take a better look at her. Sam nodded. Matt slowed for another look before abruptly hopping into a quickstep to keep up with Sam.

"Probably shouldn't even listen to Maier," Shayera said, eyes narrowing as she followed the backs of the two boys leaving. "No matter what he says he'd never do anything without Ulrich's permission."

"Because he's loyal," parroted Nate.

"Because he's not that stupid." Her view shifted to him. Her toned skin looked almost gold in the late afternoon sun. Her black tank top showed off the curve of her shoulders, as it always did, every time he'd seen her. Maybe she didn't own any other clothes. "Ulrich is the High Councilor," she continued, "everyone knows it and everyone follows. Maier is, and I hate that I'm saying this, all bark."

"So what's the point in arguing?"

"It's our way," Shayera answered, as though it was the most obvious thing in the world. "We question each other, argue, yell, and scream. That's what leads to consensus. In the end, we work together as a community. We are loyal. It's our nature."

Nate turned away. His focus caught on a pair of men walking toward the fountain. They both wore trucker caps so low they touched their eyebrows. The tall one had his hands in his pockets. The shorter kept them crossed in front. They rounded onto the path to walk away from the fountain, away from the bench where Nate and Shayera sat.

"The only way any of us survive is together." Shayera said. "Maier knows this. Ulrich too. We all know this. Well, maybe not Zarker, but he follows, mostly."

"What happened the other night? After I left with Mr. Clarkson?"

Shayera paused a moment. "No one wanted a fight," she said.

"I doubt that," Nate replied. He saw Dove's gesture again, the fake gunshot mimicking that which caused Riley's very real injuries. She was still dealing with those same injuries today, months after Remy's body was burned by . . . someone . . . to cover up the evidence. "I could smell the blood," Nate pressed, "what happened?"

"I'm not even sure myself," Shayera's eyes shut in recall. "We kept them back as you were leaving, but Zarker hurt one of them, bad." Her eyes opened again. "Brother Boniface was furious and Zarker . . . I had to shove him away from the rest. Dove wasn't even there anymore."

Nate clenched his jaw. She'd only been there to antagonize him. Provoke him, or maybe any of them, into attacking.

"I managed to get Zarker to follow me into the woods in order to lose them. I don't even know what happened to the one who'd been wounded. It was . . . bad, but they do heal very well. I ran so fast that I didn't notice when Zarker wasn't with me. He must've gone another way home. Wasn't until the next morning when I heard about these." She gestured toward the fountain where the news reporter had been. "The murders."

"You sure Zarker went home?"

"He's not vicious," she replied. "He acted in defense. Your defense." She shook her head as though in disbelief. "He wouldn't just go after an innocent person like that."

Nate looked at her incredulously.

"He wouldn't," she said again. "I know him."

"And if he killed one of them?"

"Then the Order will take it up with the

Council. Or they will try confronting Zarker about it. But I hope they have more sense than that. He's not the . . . social type."

Nate gave her a confused look.

Shayera lowered her foot from the bench. "Zarker is what we call feral. It means he prefers to live outside of society." She pointed vaguely to her left, the south of the town. "There's a few others he tends to hang around with in abandoned cabins and lumberyards, stuff left behind when the forest was declared a preserve." She looked over to him. "Your dad helped do that, ya know?"

"I know," Nate said, recalling the many times his mother told him that story on their way to Patrick Wallace Creek.

"That's actually part of why the preserve was created," Shayera said, "for people like Zarker, who think the only way to live as they're meant to is in nature. They think being true to themselves means never hiding who they are." She chuckled lightly. "He hates looking like one of them. I think that day in the parking lot was the first time I'd seen him like that in years."

Nate nodded. "He looked like it," he said.

"It was pretty bad, wasn't it?" Shayera replied. "He's not used to wearing clothes. Actually he was most disappointed that day because changing messed up his hair." She chuckled lightly. "It takes a lot to get him away from the forest. We have to signal him to come into town."

"Was there a meeting that day?"

"No, he was just visiting." Her eyes stared off. "It had been a while since . . . " Her gaze lowered, her smile vanished. "He's not a bad guy," she resumed, "he's just . . . proud."

Nate cocked his brow at this.

"Things have been quite busy since your turning. He's had to come in a lot lately."

"Is that bad?"

Shayera cocked her own brow. "It's best not to spend too much time around some people," she said. "We've learned this."

"Oh," Nate replied in surprise, "you and he were—"

"Feral," she said, cutting him off. "I tried it for a while, but it wasn't for me. People like Zarker enjoy the more savage parts of life. They like the power and what they call the freedom of not having to share a living place with . . . " She waved her hand to where others were around the park. " . . . them," she said ominously. "They like hunting prey, sleeping in the elements, shitting wherever they please, things like that." She contained a laugh before continuing. "They're respectful of the Council, of course, but you know, outside of it . . . "

"Then laws mean nothing to him."

She let out a frustrated sigh. "Zarker can't even stand the smell of humans. I can guarantee he wouldn't want it smeared all over him. That encounter the other night was the most aggressive I've ever seen him be with a person. If one of the blackrobes was injured or, whatever, then that's their fault. They know the risk. And Zarker acted out of protection, no matter what they might say." She looked over the paved center of the plaza. "The Code is lenient on protection," she added. "But Zarker wouldn't go hunting for humans. Besides," she said conclusively, "no white hair."

"All right," Nate said, "got it."

Shayera visibly eased on the other side of the bench.

"What about you?" he asked. She spun to face him, brow furrowed in offense. "You can't honestly think that I would have—"

"I mean, being feral," Nate said, hands up in front of him.

"Oh," she replied, relaxing, "I thought you meant . . . " She waved away the thought. "Anyway, no. I prefer buying meat that's ready to cook instead of gnawing on it raw and bloody." She shrugged. "Some of us want different things, I guess. The trick is to make them all work."

"So what do you call what my mom did?" he asked.

He looked over at Shayera when she didn't answer.

"Your mother . . . " she started. "Your mother's a bit different. She . . . " She paused again before shaking her head. "She did what she thought was right at the time."

"That's what she said," he replied. An imaginary laugh track entered his mind as he remembered the conversation they'd had in the living room before he'd gone to the train tracks.

"Then I think you should trust her," Shayera replied. "Anyway," she said, slapping her hands on her lap, "report's over. There doesn't seem to be any rioting. Looks like we've done our job for today."

"Is that what we were doing?"

"As far as the Council knows, it was." Shayera stretched as she stood. She was lean and stream-lined, her human form mimicking her wolf one.

"Come on," she said as Nate stood up as well. "Let's get a burger, or something else we don't have to kill." She tilted her head in a mischievous way. "The best part of living in society is our right to be lazy."

# CHAPTER 3

"THE VOICE OF ABEL'S BLOOD CRIED FROM THE ground, and the Lord commanded that the ground Cain worked would no longer yield him its strength."

Virgil kept his hands behind his back as he walked. The shadows of the passage grew and withdrew from him like the tide on the shore. Riley followed, half listening.

"Cain became a fugitive and wanderer. His punishment was too great. He told the Lord that the first person who found him would kill him. Thus the Lord put a mark on Cain that anyone who killed him would have vengeance taken on him sevenfold."

She saw him look over his shoulder toward her.

"How familiar are you with the scriptures?" he asked.

"I saw *Noah*, the Aronofsky one," she answered. "*Requiem for a Dream* was better."

"Hmph," he snorted. "Your father taught you none of this?"

"He did," Riley said, her eyes drifting down, "but it was a long time ago."

Virgil nodded. He continued forward, in the direction of the office with the ornate armoire and stone slab of a desk.

"Cain left for the Land of Nod in the east. There he built the city of Enoch, named for his son." Virgil opened the door and stepped into the office. "This displeased God. Humans were never meant to gather in large numbers."

Riley followed him. He closed the door after she entered. The room went completely black.

"We were meant to be out among creation, not packed into cities where sin could run rampant among the people."

She waited to see how much her eyes would adjust. There was no change.

"This rash of sin, beginning from the moment Cain spilled his brother's blood, caused God to see all flesh as corrupt."

Riley blinked rapidly. The room lit up in front of her. The stones were clear, distinct gaps marked where one stacked upon another. Without shadow, the ridges of the armoire flattened, but she could see the grain lines in the wood as clearly as the separation between mountains and sky.

Virgil motioned for her to sit. "His beautiful world had been—"

Riley stopped to look at the remnants of paint over the spectrum of gray on the stone wall. An outline appeared in reds and yellows and oranges and mixtures that she couldn't name. Her mind filled in the gaps between the specks of color into one large circle with another contained within it. A series of triangles surrounded the smaller circle while pointing to the outer. Other colors formed an irregular rim around the outer circle, possibly letters or some nebulous shape like that carved into the armoire. She leaned in closer. Anything more than the darkest traces of red had been invisible to her before.

"Sister Sapphira."

Virgil sat in the chair behind the stone table, his back straight and his hands folded neatly in front of him. He gestured toward the chair once more.

"How familiar are you with the Great Flood?"

"It was in *Noah*," she replied, sitting easily.

His look was one of fading patience. She folded her hands and straightened her back.

"Then you know that God chose to destroy Man so that He may start again . . . "

Riley couldn't help wondering how old Virgil was, how long he had been with the Order, when he started, how, and why. And what about Dove? She looked like she could be in her early thirties. Did their healing affect age as well? Perhaps she was in her sixties and Virgil his eighties or nineties. Would she age the same way? In ten years would she still look seventeen? Or twenty-two, as most people said?

During all the time she'd spent down in this structure over the last two months, she'd never once seen Virgil fight, train, use a weapon, or move in any aggressive way. He only walked. She tried to imagine him launching into the air the way Dove did, the thin, white ponytail swinging at takeoff and spinning through a somersault. He'd probably have the hood up though; otherwise he'd be exposed.

Her eyes wandered to one sleeve of his gleaming white shirt. The color faded to an outline, the way it had after her first drink of the blood. She saw veins and movement of forearm muscles as he gestured while speaking. The letters she'd seen before had faded into nothing but tiny lines. Ropey muscles traced his arm and shoulder, impressive for a man his age. Whatever age that was.

"Sister Sapphira?"

Riley jolted her view up to him. Outward cracks led from his eyes. They were clear in front of her, the dim candlelight flickering in a pale blue, while hers, she knew, were covered in shadow.

"I recognize that you're disinterested in our teachings," he said, as though forcing himself into patience, "however, you must know precisely what your duty is. How can you survive the dark if you remain ignorant of the light?"

"Okay," she said, trying to suppress her doubt, "what is it?"

"The curse of Cain, Sister Sapphira. The specter of Man's first corruption. The vengeance of God returned sevenfold."

She tilted her head at him.

"The flood did not rid the world of sin. We were made resilient, even against our Creator. Those who survived, the exiled descendants of Cain, their evil mixed with the other beasts not worthy of a place in paradise. They became feral. They became the evil we now fight."

Riley blinked away. She saw every minuscule line scratched into the stone floor over the years. Rock was hard, but it didn't heal.

"Riley," Virgil said. The sound of her name called her into eye contact. "I need to know that when the time comes, when you are face-to-face with an evil you had never before imagined, you will be able to do what must be done, willing to be the sword of God where His hammer failed."

She looked at the lines carved outward from the corners of his eyes. "I thought we were shepherds," she said. "Guardians."

"Times have changed, sister," he replied without hesitation. "The wolves have demonstrated their willingness to discard the conditions of the Accord."

She titled her head once more.

"The Nobilitate Nobis Accord. An agreement between the Church and the pagan wolves, the Canaanites, that neither side would seek to harm the other."

Riley shook her head as if to say she'd never heard of this before.

"Our Order is the enforcement wing of the Accord. This position allows those of suitable rank to use the blood of the wolf so that we may be their equal." Riley shuddered at the memory of hot, metallic liquid stinking up her mouth and throat, and the smell of old coins seeped through her nose. It was awful, yet had given her so much. "For a time we had good relations with the wolves of this area. Your father had frequent audience with their leader and would personally receive sacrament from him. We were assured a steady stream of blood for our members. However, our supplies have dwindled since their leader's passing. We have been forced to ration, to be selective in our membership. It was this very problem that killed your father."

"It was an aneurysm that killed him."

"An aneurysm caused from his withdrawal from the blood."

Riley flexed her jaw.

"Our duties come with tremendous power, but with that power comes dependency. Your father's body, all of our bodies, sustain such trauma that we need the blood to survive just as much as the Canaanites do."

"Maybe you should have told me this before I drank."

"Would it have stopped you?"

Riley looked away, disgusted.

"Look at what you have accomplished in your first days. You've been spared months of struggling to recover only a fraction of what had been lost. It's because of us, because of the blood, that you are now more yourself than you ever were before. More than you could have been without us." He leaned back in his seat. "It was only one dose," he said. "You can still withdraw if you wish."

Riley rubbed where one of the breaks had been in her leg. She would still be in the cast, on the crutches, wincing at every shake or twitch from her hip down. Perhaps it was selfish to want that, but she remembered her last recovery. A twelve-week sprain was bad enough; a yearlong break was so much worse. Remy came to mind, hanging from the car floor turned to ceiling. The blood was thick over his face, dripping from his hair. He was so fragile. They all were. She was lucky she still had the leg.

"What about Dove?" she asked. Virgil furrowed his brow. "Her leg. I know there are limits to our healing, but I've seen prosthetics now. She could have a spring there if she wanted it."

"The drafters of the Accord knew that as technology grew, humanity would be exponentially more powerful, thus creating an imbalance. It was decided that our Order would be restricted to technology available at the time of signing."

Riley pictured the weapon racks along the wall, swords, daggers, old pistols, and long rifles. They seemed silly in a time when any sociopath with a driver's license could legally obtain an AR-15. Or when people could continue buying more guns even after being put on trial for murder. The rule made as much sense as any other.

"The idea was that a symbiotic relationship would encourage cooperation."

She'd never seen anything like their standard wrist blade outside of video games before, but that didn't mean the technology didn't exist at the time.

"However, the wolves have violated this trust," Virgil said. "Further, they have shown no inclination toward punishing those responsible for the recent tragedies. Thus it falls upon us to fulfill our duty."

"What does that mean?"

"We're going to request that the guilty party step forward. If they refuse, then we will serve justice in accordance with our faith."

Riley waited for him to continue before shrugging.

"An eye for an eye."

"You're going to kill them?"

"A life for a life."

Riley shook her head sharply. "I'm not killing anyone."

"And I'm not asking you to," he replied. "I only ask that you be there to see exactly what we're dealing with—the evil that permeates through their being, why the Accord was necessary, and why we are the only ones able to uphold it. Maybe then you'll finally understand why many find strength in their faith."

She squinted at him, more as a way to show displeasure than an attempt to see him more clearly. He was already completely clear.

"Once you come face-to-face with evil, Sister Sapphira, you will pray for good."

# CHAPTER 4

THE WAITRESS WIPED HER BROW AS SHE RACED from the table near the door to the one next to the window. She swerved quickly to avoid the man who started to stand just as she walked by. "Thanks for coming," she said, spinning to face him and the rest of his party, not stopping her rush toward the other table. The leaving group of three passed another group of four that was already moving to replace them.

Nate continued to survey the room, from the two thoroughly overwhelmed waitresses and one less-overwhelmed waiter, to the cashier in the back of the restaurant. Order tickets lined the kitchen window. Only one chair remained empty. He'd never seen Antonio's so crowded before. The pizza was good, easily the best in town—which wasn't saying much since he could only think of four other places that sold pizza, and one of those was the gas station, with their boxes of microwavable dough. Maybe it was busy because it was Saturday, or maybe because everyone wanted to get out and enjoy that last bit of summer before the swift cooling to fall and the frozen winter. Or maybe because they were all terrified to stay home after what happened to the Baileys three nights before.

"It's gonna be a weird year," Craig said, chewing on the last bit of toppings from his third slice of pepperoni. "Dawn What's-'er-face and the boyfriend's whole family. Crazy stuff."

"There's probably gonna be a service for them or something," Tony added.

Nate watched as they spoke: Craig on the bench next to him, Tony on the other side of the table.

Between the three of them were the last two slices of an extra-large pepperoni—both Nate's pieces. A thick ring of condensation surrounded the base of Nate's drink, while all that was left of Craig's and Tony's glasses were stacks of ice cubes melting into diluted brown liquid. Craig took a bite of his crust.

"Too religious," he said, dipping the crust into the container of sauce next to the pizza.

"The hell are you doing?" Tony said.

"What?"

"That." Tony pointed at the container. The thick sauce stuck to the side of the plastic.

"That's what it's for," Craig said, biting off the sauced end of the crust.

"I know that, moron, but don't bite and then dip. I don't need to taste your spit."

"I dipped the other end, idiot." Craig bit off more crust, no sauce, as though this action proved his innocence.

"Whatever," Tony replied. "I bet Wilson reads a poem again. Probably a longer one since it was two students this time." Nate peered up at Tony. "Instead of just . . . " Tony trailed off.

"How is she?" Craig asked before stuffing the last bit of crust into his mouth. "Riry," he added.

"Seems fine. Recovering, I guess," Nate said, putting aside the fact that they hadn't talked in almost a week, since that morning in front of her apartment building, before he learned of Dawn Musgrave's murder.

Tony nodded, his eyes cast down at one of the greasy, crumpled napkins on the table.

"She does PT two or three times a week now, so that's probably something," Nate continued. Maybe that was why she hadn't replied to the last couple of texts he'd sent. She did need time to recover.

"PT?" Craig asked.

"Physical therapy."

"Oh."

"Yeah," Nate said. His eyes drifted toward the center of the table. Grease stains dotted the paper in shapeless blobs tracing the slices between pieces of pizza. "She told me it's mostly pool work for the last couple weeks." One rough line marked where the pizza cutter broke through the paper. "Kicking against the wall. Treading water. Things like that." Light brown, almost yellow drops on the white cover. "Whatever she can do to regain strength in her leg." Round drips. Some flowing together into larger pools. "Should recover, but . . . " Red-tinged water from the tomato sauce mixed with it. " . . . may never be the same again." Drips pooling. "After what happened."

"Hey," Craig waved his hand near Nate's face.

"Yo." Nate looked over to him.

"But she's okay, right?"

Nate nodded.

"Then that's good. I mean, sucks that she's hurt and really sucks about her boyfriend, but Riley's like, crazy strong."

"Yeah," Nate said, eyes returning to the red sauce, the grease stains.

"Besides, lockers are on the first floor this year, so it's the best time to be on crutches."

He gave Craig an annoyed look.

"Got it, sorry," Craig said, nodding. He pointed at the last two slices. "Yours, man."

Nate shook his head.

"If you don't want 'em . . ."

Nate waved one hand in dismissal.

"Cool," Craig said, reaching for one of the last slices.

Tony stared like a hound begging for scraps.

"Go ahead."

"Thanks. Sorry for saying—"

Nate shook his head. Tony tore into the last slice. Nate heard their chewing. Wet sounds leaped from Craig's maw and his lips pulled back, teeth out for another bite. They left jagged marks behind.

Everywhere he looked were people—regular humans, as far as he knew, whom he'd been surrounded by all his life—tearing into their food like predators into a kill, laughing and smiling. The sounds of their teeth cutting, shredding, and gnawing echoed in his mind. Red sauce and drops of grease. He sniffed at the air, smelled the spices of the sauce, the meat, and the baked dough. He had loved these smells every time he walked by, or when he and Riley came for a couple of slices before matinees at the Oak Street Cinema.

His eyes tracked throughout the crowded shop. The chewing became an undulating pulse in his ears. He sniffed at the air again. Pizza smell and nothing more. Of course, that was all. No way to tell if the people around him were people or his people, another type of people he didn't even know existed until a couple of months ago. Now they seemed to be everywhere. And they all knew him.

Nate's eyes met another pair at the last table before the bathrooms. The man in the trucker cap looked away quickly. He could have been one of the guys Nate had seen in the plaza the day before. The man took a long sip from his drink, swallowed, and said something to the guy on the other side of the table from him, who also wore a trucker cap along with a slick, black windbreaker. The second man turned to look at Nate as well. Their eyes met.

Nate nodded.

The man looked away. Both of them did. They took a moment before speaking as the waiter dropped off their check.

Nate knew he wouldn't be able to pick up their scent, not from here, not like this. He sniffed the air anyway. Instinct. They could have been his people or the other kind of people. Us or them. No way of knowing. And that was the problem.

"You keep doing that," Nate heard from across the table. He looked over to see Tony staring at him.

"What?"

"That," Tony said, lifting his nose to sniff the air. "Did you fart or something?"

Nate rolled his eyes.

"I'm kidding, man, lighten up."

"A lot going on," Nate said.

A large party rose from a pair of tables pushed

together in the middle of the dining area. They blocked the two men from Nate's sight.

"Oh yeah," said Craig, "so Matt told me you were at the park the other day."

Nate shot a harsh look to his friend.

"When one of those reporters was out there."

Tony shoved the last bit of pizza into his face.

Nate felt himself beginning to scowl. "What about it?"

"Nothing," Craig replied, placing his hands out innocently. "He just said you were sitting on a bench with some hot chick and was wondering if I knew anything about that."

Nate laughed once.

"So . . . anything I should know about that?"

The standing group lingered around their table. Nate tried to see around them as they figured out how much to tip.

"Hot chick?" Tony asked after swallowing.

"Yeah, Matt said she looked like a model or something."

"Damn. You got any pictures?"

"Old friend of my parents," Nate replied as several people wandered through his peripheral vision.

"Couldn't be that old if she's hot," said Tony.

"Wish I had friends like that." Craig sat back before continuing, "Instead, I'm stuck with your ugly butts."

Tony breathed as though about to speak before Craig interrupted. "And that wasn't meant to be literal. Like my calling you butt-ugly doesn't mean you actually have an ugly butt."

Tony leaned back with his hands up. "Hey, nothing wrong with checking out my butt, just don't call it ugly."

"Not my fault."

Only drink cups and a couple of grease-stained paper plates remained at the last table before the bathrooms.

Nate spun around to see the door behind him. Maybe the men had followed the large group. He hadn't noticed how many people passed by. The two waitresses had already started clearing off the large table, piling the group's refuse onto one table before splitting the pair apart and dividing the seats. The other table, where the men had been, was left untouched. Nate looked at the door again.

He didn't know why he'd honed in on those two guys. Probably because he'd made eye contact with one, but that wasn't an uncommon occurrence. Accidental eye contact happened all the time, to everyone, everywhere. Didn't mean anything. Still, something about those two in particular felt important, on a subconscious level. He had a sense about them.

The waiter finally got around to wiping down the table and removing the drinks and plates. They must have left.

"—that guy'll come back or something."

"Maybe. Never know with people like that."

Nate turned to find both Tony and Craig staring at him. "What?" he said.

"Those people from a while ago," Craig said. "What happened with them?"

"With who?" Nate asked, despite knowing exactly who Craig was talking about.

"The crazy guy and the lady who kicked my dad. He had a bruise on his chest for like two weeks."

Virgil and Dove, that first night, outside of Craig's house.

"Seriously?"

"Yeah, he said it was like he'd been hit by one of those nonlethal beanbags."

Virgil had known exactly where Nate would be that night. Riley as well. No way to tell how long he'd been following them. Long enough that he and Dove had known how to shepherd him to the spot where he'd see the accident happen.

They probably knew where he was right now. With his friends, among these people, laughing between bites and sips and talking loudly at their tables. Could have been Brother Boniface in the trucker cap. Nate hadn't seen what Boniface or any of the others actually looked like, only what they smelled like. No way of knowing if they were the same person, not when he was like this. The two men only left after he'd acknowledged them. He looked over the other diners once more. Potential blackrobes, potential allies, and potential witnesses.

"We should go," Nate said.

"Dude, we're kidding. That guy probably couldn't even get a grenade, let alone throw it in here."

"Well, I'm bored. I wanna get outta here," Nate said.

"All right, man, whatever you say. Head back to my place?"

"Sure," Nate replied as he started to slide across the bench.

"Tony? Wanna game, or tired of constantly getting owned?"

"I had you last time."

Nate stood. None of the other diners seemed to notice him getting up to leave.

"Hey, maybe that's why your butt is so ugly. 'Cuz I'm constantly kicking it."

"Dude, it was like fifty-fifty last time."

Nate maneuvered around the extra chair that had been added to the booth next to the door.

"How was everything today?" asked the waiter as Nate turned toward the short passage to the exit.

"Great," Nate said without stopping.

The waiter stepped into the passage in front of Nate.

"What about your friends?" he said, shuffling back to keep himself between Nate and the door. "How do they feel about their experience?"

Nate looked back to where Craig and Tony were still talking. "Fine," he replied.

"Good," said the waiter with a nod. He was a bit shorter than Nate, but thicker in the chest and arms. Some pudge pushed out the belly of his red and black long-sleeved shirt with a name tag that read "John." "We look forward to seeing you again," he said, staring directly at Nate. "Very soon."

Nate heard Tony and Craig continue to yammer. John stood with his back to the exit, wide enough that Nate couldn't comfortably squeeze past.

"Can't come back if you don't let us leave," Nate said, waving for the waiter to move.

"Maybe with your mother next time." Faint crow's feet extended from John's eyes, narrowed by heavy lids above and pulled by purplish bags beneath. Gray hairs dotted his sideburns. "We'd love to catch up with her."

"What did you say?" Nate whispered.

"Your mother. The High Councilor."

Nate scowled at him. He noticed John's right hand shaking.

"We haven't seen her in a while."

"What's going on?" Craig said from a couple feet behind Nate's shoulder. "He coming with us or something?"

John tilted his head. "Do they know?" he asked, eyes still focused on Nate's, intense as a spotlight shining right into him.

A burning began in the back of his jaw. Nate tried to imagine cool air entering his body, filling him with every breath, as Ulrich had taught him.

"How would they react?" John said quietly, staring at Nate as though trying to look through him. "How would any of these people react?"

"The hell is going on?" Craig said, probably to Tony. Nate didn't see them. All he saw was John, this random waiter, standing in front of the door. He felt his lip beginning to tremble as the heat gathered in his throat. He pictured Ulrich in the rear gallery of the museum. "Controlled breath," he'd said, "remain calm."

"That's right. Let the beast out," John said, stretching his arms to block Nate from the exit. "Let them see what you are."

"Dude, we paid!" hollered Craig. "Move outta the way!"

"The hell's going on?" asked Tony from the rear of where they'd bunched in front of the exit.

"Be a shame if they found out, wouldn't it?"

Nate's hands and shoulders burned. He tasted metal between his teeth. Even the cold he imagined entering his body grew hotter. No, he thought, not here.

"Break that little code of yours."

"You're not getting a good tip!"

"That's right," John said, as though speaking directly into Nate's skull. "We know everything about you. We know your rules, your names, where you live, your habits, your family and friends."

"The hell are you doing?"

Nate felt a push from behind.

"Let's go already!"

"Stop!" Nate shouted at his friends without turning. It came out as a growled slur.

"We can get you anytime, Nathaniel."

"Dammit, move already!"

"Anytime we want."

There was another push from behind. Tony or Craig trying to get through.

"Stop pushing me," Nate shouted.

"Then get him to move!"

Other murmurs filtered into the narrow path. The crowd in the rest of the restaurant had taken notice of the three teenagers being barred from leaving, as though they'd stolen silverware or used fake money to pay or any other thing that could be blamed on them. A couple of patrons had phones raised in front of them as if they were about to catch an act of police brutality from the side of the road.

"You're never safe," John whispered. "You or anyone you care about."

The fire spread through Nate's ribs and lungs. He thought of Ulrich again, how calmly he'd spoken of control. He thought of his mother rushing from the living room as her "condition" returned. He thought of Zarker bounding into the woods. His breaths were now heat flowing from him. Not here. Not now.

"Like we did your father."

His lips lifted into a snarl.

"Dude, just—" Craig shoved hard at Nate's side as he angled to move in front.

There was a metal click just before John shot a fist at Craig's abdomen. The hand pulled back with a red streak. A whir stashed the blade back under John's sleeve.

Craig fell sideways against the wall. He clutched his side.

"What the hell!" he yelled, staring at the blood on his palm in disbelief. His eyes were full moons of shock and fear. "What the hell!" he yelled again.

Noises poured in from the other side of the room. Nate started to turn but kept his head down instead. Better no one saw him as he tried to contain the beast.

"Never alone," John whispered quietly. "Never safe," he said louder, "We're always watching"—louder—"always with you." He stared into Nate's eyes as though taking aim. "You and all the others."

Nate heard his words like they were gunshots. He roared and felt a flash of searing pain rip through his body as his bones stretched and realigned. Thousands of needles pierced his flesh. His clothes shredded. A smoking red mass emerged in front of him.

Nate shot both arms forward. The red shape of John flew backward. The metal door frame dented on impact. The glass shattered around him. John staggered to the sidewalk outside, groaning. Blood wafted from large shards stuck into his neck and back and shoulders. Sweat beaded on his forehead. His wrist was leather and metal with traces of blood as well.

The door flew back from Nate's push. It hit the outside of the entrance and broke off the hinges. Nate angled to fit through. He pushed his shoulders back as he exited the restaurant. The street was a blur of differing odors, with only one standing out, pulsating in Nate's head.

John was a scorching red mass as he backed away down the sidewalk. The trace of blood on his wrist matched that coming from within the restaurant entryway where Craig—his friend, who had nothing to do with this, yet twice had been drawn in for no damn reason—lay clutching his side in pain and shock. For no reason other than being Nate's friend. Like Riley was. Or Remy to her. Innocents whose only crime was being close to him.

John stumbled as he retreated, hand clamped over the blood dripping from his neck. Dove had retreated too, hours before an entire family was murdered in their own home. Dawn Musgrave, Liam Bailey, his father, mother, and brother. He barely even knew any of them. They should have been left alone in their ignorance. Instead they'd been drawn into this fight.

Nate heard John's pulse pounding in the back of his mind. The world around him started to take shape: car exhaust, rubber, electricity, trash, heat from the road, paper, sweat, the cool and neutral colors of dead things, the warm ones of the living. He focused on John, still staggering away like a wounded animal.

He said they knew where Nate was all the time. That they knew the names of every one of his people. His people. Who did that include? They'd already attacked him on the street in front of his friend's house. They'd lured him into witnessing a fatal accident. He felt the skin over his fingers breaking. They'd followed him while he was out with his friends on a regular day. They'd stabbed his friend in daylight for no reason other than being his friend. The thick claws rounded over the top of his fingers. They'd do it again. Again and again until he finally did something to stop them. Until they brought out the beast.

Nate felt the concrete zoom under his feet as he charged ahead. The burning red form filled his vision. He roared. He slammed into John. Nate swung hard. His claws shredded through clothes and skin. Blood streaked from his fingers. The force of his blow tossed John off his feet and onto the sidewalk. His heart pumped heated blood through the wound across his chest. He crawled back on his elbows. He said something that Nate couldn't hear. One hand extended out. It waved through Nate's vision, fingers and thumb extended. Like Dove's had.

"Bang," he said.

Nate pounced once more. John's rushed breathing was beneath him. It was hot but sweet. Nate pulled his arm back for another blow. His claws tossed blood through the air.

A staccato noise broke through John's rapid breath and thumping heart. A scream rose in Nate's mind. He froze.

"Help," Nate heard from the concrete below.

"Help me!" John screamed, waving his hands around himself as he lay prone on the ground.

Voices poured in from all around. "Oh my God!" "What the hell is that?" "Call the police!" "Monster!"

Nate started to rise as the red dulled in his mind. Other figures emerged all around him. People cowered behind cars and walls and windows. He sensed a couple duck behind a shop entrance, clutching a small dog between them. A woman covered her child in the passenger seat of a car parked on the other side of the road. A dozen people scattered around one corner, peeking from behind streetlights, trash cans, parked cars, and each other. More people were farther away. The crowd had poured out of Antonio's. They stared at him, drenched in fear. All of them. Even John.

Nate backed away, lowering his hand.

"Help! Please God help me!"

They were watching him. Watching him from every angle. Some cradled their hands over their heads in hiding. Others had their hands out with little bluish-gray boxes extended. Phones. Everyone had a phone. Every phone had a camera. Every camera was proof. Proof that his kind was real. Proof that he was vicious and savage. Proof that would multiply, spread, go viral. Proof that would be everywhere in seconds. He was exposed.

Everyone would be talking about it.

There are werewolves in this town.

And they're killing people.

"Help me! Help me, please!" John yelled as he limped away slowly, one hand clamped over the shredded skin on his chest. Nate let him go.

He could still smell Craig's blood in the crowd outside of the restaurant. There was no bone dust or bile in the wound. A clean cut through the skin not meant for any real damage. Meant to put the scent of blood in the air. Nate could smell something else on Craig, too. Even he was afraid.

There were loud gasps as Nate raised his large hands as high as he could into the air. "You don't understand," he wanted to say, "that man started it. He attacked my friend. I just wanted to protect him."

What came out was harsh breaths and growls, which made those people closest to him dig deeper into their hiding places. If he was human, he could show them he wasn't a threat.

But then he'd also show them exactly who he was.

Nate turned swiftly to more gasps and cowering. He searched for the scents of trees, moss, and dirt. He found them at the very edge of his perception. He sprang in the direction of the forest. Pedestrians ran or laid flat beneath bus stop benches and car tires. Those in the shops sank to the floor or pressed themselves into tiny corners. There were screams and cries as he passed. He heard sirens in the distance.

He ran on all fours. Like the animal he was. Like the monster they saw.

No one was safe.

Not anymore.

# CHAPTER 5

THE IMAGES WERE BARELY VISIBLE THROUGH THE movement in the video—both that of the figure in the footage, as it bounded forward in off-kilter hops, and the hands holding the cameras, which were shaking more wildly than a Bourne movie during an earthquake. "Breaking News: Mysterious Attack in Alaskan Town," read the news ticker across the bottom of the screen. "Are there monsters among us?" asked the huge graphic just over the news anchor's right shoulder as the broadcast cut from one poorly filmed video to another.

The video started in the restaurant, which

the entryway and uniforms easily identified as Antonio's, capturing a group of boys being barred from the door by a waiter Riley wasn't sure she'd seen before. The moving cameras made it impossible to tell who each of the boys were before sudden shouts and a crash led to one of them falling against the wall.

Then the whole image pushed backward as though hit by a sudden hurricane.

Riley cringed at the sound of broken metal and shattered glass. The camera dropped for a few seconds as the man holding it dove to the ground before remembering that he was recording the scene. The image inched upward.

The creature had to turn and duck to fit through the door. A few spots of black mixed in among the dense layers of dark brown hair that covered wide shoulders like a series of hooks riding its back and neck. Scraps of torn clothes clung and fell from it. It seemed to wait a moment as it stepped outside, stretching its shoulders before turning into profile.

The shape wasn't what Riley had expected. There was the extended jaw and nose like that of a wolf, the ears and thick hair, a neck that looked two feet long and stuck ahead of the curved back. Its hands were big enough to wrap over the top of her head. Its arms were more than a foot thick, the biceps were covered in a downy fur, with the triceps under denser hair that swept back like tiny wings or fins. The creature seemed to pause there a moment. The side of its red eye blazed into the camera. Then the creature sprang forward in a sudden, violent motion.

Half a dozen other cameras picked up the action from here: held from the base of a window in a nearby shop, from the other side of the road, far on the opposite corner, inside a car and ducking as the creature ran by, under a different car tracking dog-like hind legs and hanging claws nearly scraping the sidewalk, and in the background as a girl filmed herself hiding behind a mailbox while confessing her love for a boy at school. The footage from inside the restaurant, the one Riley watched for the tenth time right now, was the best. It managed to catch Craig, one of Nate's friends, clutching the small wound on his stomach before the cameraman ran to the sidewalk in front of the restaurant. There the shaking stopped.

The creature—the wolf—chased down the waiter as he stumbled backward, bleeding from the glass stuck in his back. It took one swing, which cut across the waiter's chest and tossed him to the ground. People screamed as the wolf jumped on top of the waiter. It raised back one stump-like arm to strike. The camera zoomed in. The claws were several inches long and dripping blood. The screaming continued. The creature stopped.

Its head rose to sniff the air as though just now becoming aware of the people around it. The waiter cried for help while scrambling up to his feet. No cameras followed him as he ran off. The wolf raised its hands. The span of its arms looked nearly as long as the compact car parked on the road behind it. The camera on the opposite corner caught the slits of its red eyes, the previous glow fading into a duller color. Its face was almost exactly that of a dog except more angular, sharper around the edges, with patches of fur extending from its chin and under its short, pointed ears. It let out sounds as though trying to speak. Then it hunched forward, steadied itself, and sprang ahead, clearing half the street in a single hop.

It disappeared in a second.

"Disturbing videos from Stumpvale, Alaska," said the anchorman as he reappeared on screen, "where an altercation caused a young man to transform into this . . . creature, I don't even know what to call it." He shook his head in what looked like a practiced confusion, as though feigning shock were his default reaction. "Joining us now, live from the town of Stumpvale, is Rebecca Egde, who has been covering . . . "

The creature hesitated for a moment before running away, as though it knew it had made a mistake. It didn't even kill the waiter while he lay helpless beneath it. The man ran away and, according to the news, had yet to be found. There had been so much power in the way the wolf sped down the sidewalk and sliced the man's chest with a glancing blow that still threw the waiter backward.

The argument in the restaurant didn't seem so bad. Yet, this otherwise normal person decided to expose himself as this . . . thing . . . this cursed creature. Why would something that strong, something that powerful, be so afraid of a little waiter that he, that it, would allow itself to be caught transforming in front of what he must have known were witnesses? Almost as though he wanted to be seen. He wanted to spit in the face of the Accord between wolves and humans.

"And why not?" she imagined Virgil would ask. Hadn't they already started breaking those rules? They'd literally gotten away with murder.

A gray-haired man with tiny glasses and a brown sports coat appeared on the screen next to another man with balding hair and a goatee. The bald one gestured grandly as he spoke. The other shrugged and went quiet. Didn't matter what they were saying. They didn't know anything. Riley was sure of that.

And how could they? They'd spent their entire lives sheltered from the reality of the monsters who walk among them. Hidden the way she had been until one of these creatures, a part of their corruption, forced itself into her life in the most brutal way possible, by taking someone just as innocent as they were. As innocent as she had been before then.

The waiter was lucky to be alive. He could easily have been torn to pieces like the Baileys were, decapitated like Dawn. The others on the street were lucky as well. They were sheep at the mercy of the wolf. Unknowing, going about their regular day of eating pizza or shopping or driving from one place to another—places where they were meant to feel safe—when something so much larger, so much more powerful, so far out of their control just . . . happened around them. It was like an invasion. A violation not only of some secret agreement but of the rules which allow anyone, human and wolf, human and human, to live together. No one should ever have to live in fear that those around them have the power and will to murder them on a whim. Yet here it was, happening right in front of her. In front of the entire world. A random, sudden danger. A danger that could happen at any time or any place. A danger that normal people, the everyday folks who lived in this town, lived in every other town and city around the world in which wolves lived in secret, could never defend themselves against. This is why the Order was created. Order. Control. To keep random, chaotic things from happening.

Riley rubbed at the back of her leg. The scar rose from it like a hilltop. She glanced at the hand that touched the lines on the side of her face, saw down the arm to the indents that shaded her arm.

This wolf was a threat. They all were. And they were everywhere. All of them deadly. All of them able to kill, easily. They already had. This could have been a warning. They are tired of hiding. They want the world to know that they exist. That they are strong. That their mood decides who will live and who will die.

They'd only become bolder from here on. More dangerous. Deadlier. It didn't even matter why this wolf, this creature, had chosen to react as it did. A weapon is a weapon no matter its intent. A gun doesn't care who fires it or why. It just kills. What she saw replayed before her in slow motion, from half a dozen angles, was a living weapon. Weapons needed to be defended against. They needed to be kept from those who would use them to harm others. This wolf, who'd tossed a helpless waiter through the door of Antonio's, had already shown a capacity to harm. He'd already used his curse. Like the one who killed Dawn and Liam and Liam's family, and even one of her own brothers just three nights before. The one who'd been on the road that night while she and Remy drove harmlessly down a road they'd traveled hundreds of times before. Assuming it was only one.

She had felt safe that night, before the sudden swerve that sent her rolling like a cannonball made of metal and glass. Felt like nothing could happen to her. Nothing like that, at least. Sprains and bruises and even breaks, but those would heal. Those were temporary. But death . . . that wasn't something she'd had to worry about. One day, but not yet. Not while she was growing and becoming who she was meant to be. Her father was older, set, and settled when he died. He was vulnerable. She was still figuring out how to live. She was invincible.

Then she wasn't.

And she'd never be safe again.

Neither would any of those around her: her friends, her mother, her teachers, everyone watching this report right now. This wolf, one of the Canaanites as Virgil called them, was bad, bad enough to kill. Bad things, bad people, can't be trusted with power. It makes them dangerous.

Dangerous things must be contained. They must be regulated by those capable of regulating them.

Riley felt herself beginning to shake as she stared at the video replaying once again in front of her. She tensed the muscles in her leg. They felt strong. They felt healed. She felt ready.

# CHAPTER 6

**T**HERE WAS A LOUD KNOCK ON THE DOOR.

Nate bolted up like a deer hearing distant gunfire. He dug his fingers into the armrest of the couch. His mother patted his shoulder. "It's fine," she said. "It's fine." She walked around the other side of the table, cutting through Nate's view of himself, the other version of himself, putting his huge, hair-covered hands out and hesitating before running from the town.

His mother pushed the curtain back from the front window enough to peek out. He saw the shadow of her head against the light through the curtain.

"  . . . said to be the product of a coupling between humans and ancient animal spirits," said the man on the television, whom the anchor introduced as an "expert" on mythology and the occult.

Nate's mother leaned her head farther between the curtain and the window. Nate leaned over to look too, despite knowing that he'd never be able to see who was at the door. There was a way he could, but he wouldn't consider it, not after the sprint home, transforming in the woods, hopping over the fence, and making the final run to the backdoor completely naked.

"But here we see the creature doesn't go for the kill," said the anchor in the blue suit with the American flag pin on his lapel. "He seems distracted as the man escapes."

His mother stood a moment in contemplation.

"Who is it?" Nate whispered.

His mother shook her head. She smoothed the curtain over the window.

" . . . a warning that humans have encroached too far on their territory," said the expert. "This is meant to scare us."

His mother stepped along the wall to the front entrance, her shadow covering the light peeking through as she opened the door. She said something Nate couldn't hear. Again, there was a way he could, but not today, not when he was human, and this was no time to change again. Probably the best outcome of the entire incident was that he had completely destroyed his last pair of shoes, just as the weather was starting to cool down. Everything else was much, much worse.

" . . . suspect we'll see more of these attacks?"

"Now that we're aware of them. Yes."

The light grew as his mother stepped back to open the door wider.

"Many, many more."

Maier took a second to wipe his feet on the mat

outside before entering the house. He nodded to Nate's mom as she held the door open. She looked unamused.

"Been quite a day, hasn't it?" Maier said, unzipping his well-worn jacket.

" . . . wouldn't be surprised if we saw many more such attacks very so—"

"Samantha," Maier said, folding his jacket over his arm, "would you mind if I spoke to your son alone?"

She looked at Nate for a moment. Stones were in her eyes. She folded her arms.

"Things have changed, Samantha, more than any of us currently understand. There are concerns—"

"Anything that concerns my son also concerns me," Nate's mother replied harshly, shutting the door behind him.

"It concerns all of us, but before the hordes descend upon your boy, I'd like to speak with him honestly, and I can only do so in private."

Nate's mother stepped back and crossed her arms

once more. Maier turned, and Nate saw him in profile.

"Samantha, our disagreements were a long time ago," Maier whispered loud enough for Nate to hear. "You can't choose to isolate yourself for years and still retain authority."

"I did that for my son," she replied over the yammering of the television.

"And I understand that choice. However, your son has expressed an interest in rejoining our greater community, including taking part in confidential Council meetings."

Nate turned back to the television. There he was, shoving John through the glass door as Craig held back the blood spilling from his side. So far no one had gotten a clear shot of Nate's face. Didn't mean they weren't going to find out who he is. Especially since two of his friends were there, right next to him, in at least three different videos. Not to mention John, or whoever he was. Nate was astonished none of them had talked yet.

"Anything you have to say to him, you can say to me."

"It's okay, Mom," Nate said. There was a freeze-frame of a video shot by someone looking up from the floor of the restaurant. In the grainy cell image, Nate could see the remnants of his clothes clinging to the hair covering his shoulders. "I can handle this."

His mother's irritation was replaced with concern. It showed as deep lines in her forehead and parentheses around her mouth.

He nodded to her. "I got it."

She blinked quickly. "Okay," she said, resigned. "Guess I'll head into town for a little while. Anything you need?"

Nate shook his head.

"Town may not be the best idea right now, Samantha."

She paused a moment, facing the door, hand on the knob. "Nothing's changed for us, Ron. We've always known what we are." She opened the door without another look and walked outside. Maier pushed the door closed behind her.

On the television Nate's enormous arm swung in slow motion. Blood trailed from the sharpened tips of his fingers. "Uncontrollable," said a new voice. "Savage."

"How about we turn this drivel off?" Maier asked, one finger pointing toward the television. The short sleeves showed off solid arms, white hairs along the top of them. He stepped in front of Nate to block his view of the television. Nate held the remote out.

"This new threat must be—" The blather finally stopped.

"So," Maier said, dropping the jacket onto the coffee table in front of him. "You've become quite the sensation."

Nate hung his head. He heard the table creak as Maier sat down on it.

"What exactly is this YouTube thing?" he asked. "Can just anyone post videos there?"

Nate glanced up. Maier seemed to be talking to the covered window several feet away.

"Anyone?" he asked again. "Could be real, could be fake. Could be anything." He turned toward Nate. "But you and I know that these videos are real. The whole world knows, and by now, the whole world has seen them. Thus they know that we, our kind—you and me and your mother and all the rest—we are real."

Nate dropped his chin. He squeezed his eyes tightly. One hand went to the top of his head, fingers through his short hair, nails dug into his scalp.

"The Council was already called in, those who are available at least."

"So why are you here?" Nate asked, head still down, eyes still closed, one hand pulling the hair at the crown. The pain in the roots felt deserved. That and more.

Maier was silent for a second before, "Because I thought it was more important to talk to you than talk about you."

Nate's hand fell to his lap.

"When I left, Ulrich was in the process of gathering his fellow heads to discuss possible courses of action."

Nate looked up just enough to see Maier's bent knees where he sat on the table. "Fellow heads?" he asked.

"Head Councilors from other locations. Every city where we've settled establishes its own local body, as outlined in the Accord. Those groups have jurisdiction over what happens within their territory and outlying areas. When something happens that has repercussions outside of any one territory, well . . . "

Nate held his head in both hands, elbows on his knees.

"Our arrangement becomes more complicated."

"He stabbed my friend," Nate muttered. "He threatened everyone."

"Not according to the video. Not according to

the story that's currently racing across the entire world."

Nate swore under his breath.

Never safe, exactly as John said.

"Right now it's just phone calls. Nothing in the Accord bans us from using technology . . . "

Only a matter of time before they found out who he was. Craig could tell them, or Tony. Friendship probably didn't last when you found out your friend was a monster who could rip you in two with the flick of one razor-tipped finger. The television had been off for a couple of minutes. They could have already talked. Police helicopters and news vans could be moving this second, SWAT teams assembling in the field behind the house. They would apprehend his mother the moment she walked into the supermarket. Nate felt the dampness behind his eyelids. He should call her. Warn her.

" . . . or offer you up as a scapegoat, a lone wolf so to speak, anything to keep the rest of us from being exposed. It's a practical move."

His name and face next to footage of a horror-movie monster in a berserker rage in the middle of a crowded street. Not exactly the way he'd ever wanted to become famous. Would they try to capture him? Run tests and experiments to see what he was and how he became this? Search for practical uses for his "gifts"? Or would they simply kill him, like a dog that attacked a stranger?

"Doesn't make it any better for you or for your mom, but for the rest of us, it might be the most acceptable course of action . . . "

He dug his fingers in his scalp again. If he were to somehow pop his claws out right now, without transforming the rest of his body, would they break his skull and stab his brain? Kill him on the spot? SWAT team would break through the door and find him dead on his couch, apparent suicide. Pin the murders on him just to clear the cases. His lower lip quivered. A teardrop leaked from the corner of his left eye. At least then the others might be safe. At least that way it would be quick.

Maier continued on about the Council and Ulrich—something about making a deal for transfer or exile or other such things. Didn't matter.

Riley would find out. No way she wouldn't. Even if no one else recognized him on any of the videos which never stopped airing, she would. Maybe she was the one friend who would understand and stay with him but . . . but this wasn't exactly a secret that could be accepted. What would it be like coming out as a werewolf? He wouldn't be applauded for bravery and honesty, like when movie stars came out as gay. He wouldn't be gently tolerated, as people treated their vegan friends. He wouldn't even be written off, ridiculed, or labeled as foolish, like climate-change deniers or anti-vaxxers were. There was no pro-werewolf group, not openly at least, not that he knew of. Maybe he could be the first. And the first of any new group was always treated well. It wasn't like there was a history of early members of a population being executed or tortured, hung from trees, dragged behind cars, forced into prison camps.

No, people have always been tolerant of those different from themselves. Especially when the different ones were shown on a dozen video recordings threatening a member of the majority.

Or maybe Riley wasn't the one friend who would understand. She could put together that he'd been there that night, caused the accident, killed Remy, broken her. That the last two months of pain and frustration were his fault. Not only had he failed to protect her, he'd hurt her.

Nate's eyes opened, water trailing down his face in fat drops. "I screwed up," he said. "I screwed up so bad."

"Hey," Maier replied as though trying to be comforting, "you were in the wrong place at the wrong time with the wrong people. Regardless of the reaction, I'm sure Ulrich and the rest understand and sympathize."

The muscles in Nate's face squeezed inward at the exact same time. He collapsed forward. His breaths came out in heaving sobs. He pulled his hands over his head, the only way he knew to hide himself from anyone who could see him. Right now it was only Maier, but it would soon be the world. He couldn't breathe in fast enough to force the air back out. He tasted the salt of his tears as they streamed down his face. His panting cry, like a baby, echoed between his arms and chest.

He'd failed. No denying it. He'd failed in everything he tried to do. The Code of the Blood. The Council. Keeping his own secret. He'd failed to protect his friend from being hurt. His mother. Riley. In fact, he hadn't just failed; he'd contributed to their pain. He'd caused it. If not for him . . .

He sniffled. Closed his mouth and inhaled deeply through his nose.

If not for him . . .

"Has anyone told you about the time before the Accord?"

Nate rubbed his eyes and face before looking up. Maier stared directly at him, eyebrows raised as though awaiting an answer.

Nate shook his head.

Maier looked away for a moment, gathering his thoughts. "Ulrich and most of the others may not like to acknowledge it, but the Accord is only about two hundred and thirty years old. For far more of our species' history, we lived free of its restrictions and limits." He sighed looking at the light filtering through the curtain over the window. "There were fewer people then, of course. Not as spread out nor as tightly packed into the cities. Harder to communicate as well. No one could post on YouTube at the time." He glanced over at Nate as he said this, the foundation of a smile flashing and then disappearing when he looked back to the window. "So it was easier to live in secret, then," he nodded, "but we could live openly. Mostly on our own, in small towns like this one. We were left alone. The people nearby would know better than to infringe on our territory."

"Who told you all that?" Nate asked.

"My father did, a short time after my Feral

Right—that's the traditional first-changing ceremony. I was just a few years younger than you are now."

"It's not true," Nate said firmly. "We were hunted. Of course we were."

"If we entered their towns, yes," Maier said with a nod. "It was a dangerous time. But there's always danger." His view drifted. The kitchen, the door to Nate's mother's room, the wall of paintings. He appeared to squint at one of them. "At least then we were free to live on our own, among our own kind." His view roamed along the wall to where the staircase met the end of the living room, the back-door a few feet away. "There's no way of knowing, of course, but maybe if we had been able to exist in such a way, with our presence known, we could have reached a point by now where acceptance would be possible." Maier continued his survey of the house: the shelf of books and old DVDs, the television, the other shelf, the window. "Perhaps if we hadn't spent the last two hundred and thirty years in secret . . ."

he said. "Secrets create suspicion." He took a breath and then snapped to look back at Nate. "Just the same, there's no way of knowing what would have been since it never was."

Nate looked away, head shaking, jaw clenched. The water gathered in his eyes again.

"This was inevitable," Maier said. "Ulrich's a good leader, and I'd never do anything against his wishes, but it was obvious to anyone willing to look that the old ways wouldn't work anymore. Not in a world as connected as this one."

Nate wiped his eyes before glancing sideways at Maier.

"And definitely not after today."

Nate shook his head, fuming.

"Well," Maier said, rapping his hands on his legs. He stood up. He turned to look down at where Nate remained on the couch, the same place he'd sat since coming down from his room after getting dressed. He'd been there long enough to feel a dull ache in his legs and back. Or that might have been from sprinting through the woods for fifteen or twenty minutes.

"For what it's worth, Nate," Maier said, "I believe you about your friend being attacked. If it had been anyone else in that situation, or if you had been with one of us, a more experienced member of our community, then we wouldn't be in this situation. It seems clear to me that the blackrobes have been targeting, tormenting, and provoking you for quite some time, and that Ulrich has done everything he can to placate them as though the old ways, the ways of your father and Pius, still applied."

"Where is he now?" Nate asked. "Father Pius?"

"He died." Maier seemed to question his response for a moment before stepping around the side of the couch. He continued toward the rear wall between the living room and kitchen, looking directly at the staircase. He leaned out to see something. "Your father?" he asked, pointing vaguely toward the staircase wall.

"Yes," Nate said, looking at Maier over the back of the couch.

"He was a good leader. Traditional but open-minded. Focused on strengthening the community both inside and out." Maier lowered his head. "Everything changed after he died."

"What do you mean?" Nate asked.

Maier turned. "How did your mother tell you he died?"

"Car accident."

Maier nodded for a moment. "I can see why she'd tell you that. The same reason why she'd bring you out here, never tell you abou—"

"What happened?"

"It was the Order," Maier stated plainly. "They said it was a rogue action." He looked to the stairs again, the photos. "He managed to kill two of them but the third . . . well . . . we still see her from time to time."

"Her?"

"Yes." His eyes locked with Nate's. "Sister Dove."

Nate felt an explosion in the center of his chest. His back teeth pressed together.

"Stay strong, brother Fenrei," Maier said, "you'll need it for the trials ahead."

Nate didn't hear Maier's feet shuffle on the carpet. He didn't hear the door open and close. He heard the laugh. He heard a giddy little girl playing with a new toy. A toy that she'd made.

# CHAPTER 7

THE FOREST LOOKED LIKE IT DID AT NOON WITH-
out the overhead sun casting shadows that
darkened the ground beneath the branches and
leaves, or the strong shafts that cut between those
same shadows. Every movement was clear: the flutter of the leaves overhead in their hundred varieties
of green, the gentle sway of the branches near the
tops of the trees, the bend of the grass, the dust
kicked up from the ground, and the quick steps and
turns that caused that dust to stir and that grass to
bend, the waves in the bottom of the long fabric
covering the rest of the motion.

The creak of the wood and rustle of the leaves masked the sounds of their steps. Riley could only tell that there was any motion other than the wind when she was positioned between the others and knew what to listen for and when. From her place near the back she could see them, her brothers and sisters as they called themselves, weaving between the trees and jumping over shrubs and fallen branches. Each step was a whisper, each landing a sigh. Lighter than landing on a spring mat. She felt an effortlessness in leaping from one foot to the other as she dashed toward the trunk of a large tree. Her lunges, left or right, forward or back, were as easy on her muscles as twitching a finger or blinking. They were barely a thought. She clearly saw the tree as four feet in diameter and with a deep gash splintering several inches inward about fifteen feet up. The gash appeared more man-made than natural, as though from an axe or some other sharp object.

She took a quick stride away from the tree.

Other cloaks dashed in front of her, ducking and dodging, leaping over every obstruction under the canopy of branches. She hastened her steps to keep up, increased noise following her increased speed. The whispers grew louder on each step.

One thing she couldn't do at all was smell. There was the scent of the trees and the night air, the dirt and moss, the general forest odors she'd always notice when out in the woods, especially at night when the cold allowed moisture to form on the leaves and the rocks. But she couldn't smell her own scents: the perspiration gathering on the back of her neck from the movement and the amount of fabric covering her, or the smell of her breath bouncing back from the cloth, extending over her mouth and nose from one side of the hood to the other. In their place was nothing. She couldn't smell the cloak itself even as it wrapped around her like a blanket that concealed everything except her eyes and opened just enough for her arms and legs to move.

The trees became sparser in the distance. A clearing was up ahead. She looked around at the others: Dove, Carolyn, Virgil, and one more brother whose name she hadn't gotten. Riley could see them in her head even behind the trees, not like looking through the fabric to blades they all had strapped to their wrists, everyone except for her and Virgil, but a feeling of knowing exactly where they were by seeing where they had moved, what was around, their speed and motion. She made the pattern. A change in the way her cloak turned told Riley exactly when Carolyn would splinter off from the rest of them. She knew for the others as well. The way their rhythms altered and their clothing shifted told her exactly what they would do before they did it.

Dove continued forward as Virgil stopped about thirty feet ahead of where Riley slowed to an easy walk in a flat patch between two sets of roots. He turned back to her and nodded, but she could only see his eyes and the vertical movement of his head.

Riley nodded back. Virgil wandered to the right. He walked as though the rest of the world would wait for him.

She continued forward several more steps. The fence dividing the woods from the clearing began seventy feet in front of her, brown and brittle with signs warning them to KEEP OUT, then the open field with a few bushes, a gentle slope downward before another slope up with a pair of large rocks. A rusted and abandoned lumber storage building stood another forty feet beyond the fence. Holes had worn into the metal roof, and cracks were visible in the upper walls. She could see the stars and three-fourths of the moon as white spots in a sky that was black but cast no darkness beneath it. Riley nestled into the tall grass near a tree. She knelt down, letting her cloak settle. To an observer, she'd look as indistinct as her surroundings. Dark or light, she'd smell like nothing.

Dove had taken a similar position, crouched in what would be the dark of a tree at the very edge of the woods. To her right, between a line of trunks, Riley could see where an old gate was held together by a pair of rusty chains. If the wolves could leap the way her brothers and sisters could, there'd be no reason to ever open it. Sprouting grass marked where the woods had started to reclaim the dirt road. Virgil made his way over, walking calmly toward the fence. He paused for a moment, his back to both Riley and the fence. He removed something from the inside of his cloak, a vial with a small brush that he'd shown her a couple of weeks before. He pulled the front of his hood down as he applied a dose of concentrated pheromones. Virgil had told her that the Eye of Providence, the all-seeing eye, was originally a symbol of divinity. It meant that God was watching over all of creation. Only later was it co-opted into something more sinister by people who knew nothing of its origin. He stashed the vial and turned toward the fence. He placed his palms up as though preparing to take communion or confess his crimes. His hood hung to just above his eyelids, and his head tilted back slightly to see under it. He remained in that position, approaching with a long pause between each step.

Somewhere in this area, Virgil stated, was the one responsible for the rash of murders and panic which had swept through the town. The one who'd broken the Accord. Even if those beyond the fence refused to work peacefully, he said, Riley would at least get her first glimpse of the corruption at work. Videos from earlier that day were not enough to know the peril they now faced.

A tiny motion caught Riley's attention. Movement from within the fence, a shaking in one of the shrubs. Other spots began to stir, tall grass and bushes, shaking as if about to uproot themselves. A hand extended from the first shrub. There was no way to tell exactly how large it was, but it reached out from within the greenery, then pulled against the ground. Spike-like nails pierced the earth. The line of a jaw and snout came next, a tuft of jagged fur hanging from the chin like a beard styled into several points. The eyes struck her, red and small, blinking as they looked from one direction to another.

The creature stopped to smell the air. Its ears pointed straight up like devil horns, turned toward the entrance into the clearing. A series of sharp ends jutted off its head and down its back as it emerged from its hiding place.

Riley's mouth gaped open behind the cloth covering as the wolf stood there. Its body seemed to have no end. The curve of its head and neck led to its long back, covered with shorter hair, which led to a pair of legs thicker than the roots at Riley's feet. Finally, the beast knelt with its two legs bent beneath its weight, the hair on its thighs matted and spun into short swirls. The wolf placed one arm on the ground in front of it. Fur stuck out in long points like the gauntlet of a fantasy-movie villain.

It didn't look like the wolf from the videos she'd

been watching all day, not that any of the recordings had an especially good view, what with the motion blur, graininess, and the subject's general fear of being noticed. The short, neat fur of the wolf she'd seen in the footage looked tame compared to the odd juts and spikes of fur covering this one. It was like seeing a domestic dog compared to a wild one. She didn't know which would be more dangerous: a wolf within humanity, or a wolf without humanity. Of course, it was one thing to see a wolf as a flat, blurry image on a television, with the inherent safety of a signal beamed onto a screen. Virgil was right. It was different seeing an actual werewolf in person: sharp and three-dimensional, no comfort of distance or even the slimmest chance that all the commotion of the day had been an elaborate hoax or a bad publicity stunt.

Others crept slowly out from tall grass, bushes, and the rusted building, sniffing the air. Ten of them—no, twelve of them—no, fifteen—slithering like snakes emerging from their dens. Still no way to tell how big they were. The one in the video made Craig, a few inches taller than Riley and with extra bulk around his belly and arms, look like a child. Bigger than Dove. Bigger than Virgil.

The first wolf, the one that resembled a walking mass of sharp points, put one hand in the air. An earthquake emanated from the barrel of its chest. Riley pictured the barrels in the distillery of the Order's complex, those caked in residue from their stockpile of drained blood. Had this one contributed any of his blood to their supply? Those barrels were much smaller than the wolf's torso. How much blood would it have?

The creatures in the distance stopped their approach. Some froze just outside of the building, their heads peeking out to see what the commotion was. The first wolf continued forward, hunched over its bent legs, its arms swinging low enough that the tips of its wide fingers nearly touched the ground on every step. Its growl rolled on, the sound almost as jagged as the creature making it.

Riley looked over at the front gate into the clearing, past where a couple of other wolves had emerged from their own sleeping spots. Virgil stood completely still a few feet from the fence. His hood was up, cloak closed in front of him, and hands out from his sides in a show of passivity. The lead wolf continued forward, smelling the air as it moved. Its snarl faded with distance. Its nose wrinkled along the top and side, a fang showing under its lifted cheeks. The creature nearly recoiled from the scent. Its thick fingers appeared to grow outward. Long nails grew from its fingertips, solidifying over each end in a semitranslucent material that sharpened until Riley couldn't even see where the claw ended and the air around it began. The size of the wolf, its shape, its movement—nothing about the beast seemed natural. It didn't make sense that something like this, something so large and brutal, something out of cheesy horror movies made to look bad, could actually exist in the world. Yet here it was, only feet separating her from this . . . thing . . . this monster that looked like it could bite her in half before she'd even see its teeth. The wolf approached Virgil at the gate.

There was a blur of motion along the side of the fence. Dove dashed along the border. There was no sound other than a light flutter of the end of the cloak behind her. The rest was the wind.

They'd told Riley to remain in the back: she was still in training and should not engage. They didn't say how far back or from what angle. They'd also told her that she was there to observe, to see their enemy—Virgil had used the word enemy—up close for the first time, learn its habits and behaviors. She couldn't observe much from here. She couldn't even see her fellow guardians anymore. Better to be close to the others as she was still in training and all. Better to be within range of Dove.

Riley glanced around quickly. Nothing moved except the wind and a wisp of dust from where her cloak brushed the ground. She lifted onto her legs, not a hint of pain or resistance in them, and ran parallel to the fence.

She settled again near another tree, a good distance beyond where Dove hid. Fifty feet ahead, Virgil kept his hands out as he stepped right up to the brittle gate. Rusted barbed wire tilted outward and directly over his head. His lips were moving but his words were too quiet for Riley's ears, even now. The wolf showed bright red gums above the roots of spiked teeth. The hair fluttering gently in the wind made her remember that the points over its body weren't thorns but clumps of fur. The beast rolled its back forward, slouching ahead with arms hanging from curved shoulders and the ends of its claws poking the dirt road which cut under the gate. The broken growl continued, although she couldn't tell whether she heard the noise or imagined as it was before.

Glancing around briefly, Riley saw a few of the other wolves beginning to approach as well. One was long and lean with hair hanging in soft waves.

Another was thicker with tufts bubbling from its outline like garlic cloves. Still another had a long white stripe up its back and over its head. Most of the others remained back, withdrawn into their hiding places or peeking through the open door of the storage building. Those who approached did so with their fangs showing, claws extended, the spring of their steps powerful enough that their heads bobbed with every footfall. There were four in all. The other eleven—that she could see—stayed in place, watching as Virgil continued muttering something she couldn't quite hear.

Virgil kept his hands open as he gestured. He pulled the strings lining the front of his cloak and pushed it aside. He was exposed, but that was the point of the pheromones, a distraction so blinding that the wolves couldn't ignore it. It was to pull attention away from the others. It was also to remind them that their actions were always being watched. They were never alone. Opening the cloak, Riley assumed, was to show that Virgil was armed. It was honesty. His face was even and calm, every line clear in her sight from the shade under his hood to the collar of his gleaming shirt.

She hadn't seen herself that way, but she knew that she, like the rest of them, had impenetrable shadows covering from her brow to the top of her cheek. Virgil had told her that he'd been receiving the sacrament for so long that it no longer affected him the way it once did. Eventually it would happen to each of them, if they lived long enough. For now, they were beneath the shroud. Would that therefore make Virgil bathed in the light, as it was for the wolf?

She imagined her father in the same way. His kind eyes, a soft brown with flecks of green, the inward slope of the lids when he'd speak to her during dinner or say goodnight before she went to her room, covered in an inky black. The shadow faded from the inside out, it felt like she should be able to make out the shapes under it, even in the darkness, but it still covered everything. She doubted her father had received the sacrament long enough to have the effect fade. Especially if it was withdrawal that killed him.

The wolf's words were short and hard, a rumble too low for Riley to understand even if she could hear them. A glob of spit launched from his massive jaw. Virgil listened. As Prior, her father would've been there too, under that hood, inches from that gate, feet from the snarling, fanged beast. Is this what he'd done after she went to bed? "Sweet dreams, dear," she could hear him say. "Tomorrow will be better."

It was difficult to imagine him like this, wearing the folds of treated cloth, the cuff beneath his sleeve, the hood pulled over his head with a blazing, invisible symbol traced over it. This image of her father facing off with a hulking beast, the way Virgil was now, was not one she could have imagined before. That wasn't the father she knew. But, apparently, it was the Father others knew.

There was a loud clatter, the sound of metal

shaking. Riley looked up to see the first wolf grabbing onto the fence. Its grasp stretched the metal links. Virgil dropped his arms to his sides, kicking up dust as he slid back on the dirt path. A roar shook the leaves overhead. The wolf kicked at the fence. The points of its hair waved stiffly. Its arms tensed, pulling at the chain links. Its legs flexed, thighs bulging under the fur, planting into the ground. Its jaw snapped. The others behind charged forward.

Virgil crossed one arm to the handle of the sword hanging from his belt. "Sister!" he bellowed.

Dove popped up as a flash. Leaves and grass and dust flew behind her. She sprang off the ground and over the fence. Her cloak fluttered behind her like Superman's cape. Her landing was a muffled breath. She charged into the clearing without pause to recover.

"The others!" Virgil yelled to her. His sword was still sheathed.

The wolf yanked at the fence. The entire side

bucked back and forth. Its teeth banged. Vicious. Savage. Nothing but brutal.

Dove charged to the four other wolves closing in. She was a blur. A trail of dust and grass lined her wake. The air itself was more visible than she was. The cloak streamed back but remained closed. She couldn't have been completely invisible to them. Maybe half-formed. Like a ghost. An apparition bearing in, its ends fluttering behind. Dove's giggle started and faded into the distance.

Riley's heart thumped in her chest as she kneeled lower to the ground. Her pulse pounded through her arms and legs and into the tips of her fingers and toes. It was like electricity racing through her. But she remained still. The sharp teeth snapped at the fence. The metal clattered. Bits of rust flew off. The noise echoed in her head. The posts banged together. Thin and hollow and metallic. Like crutches. Like wreckage. She felt her hamstring tense through the cloak and the pants beneath. The long scar on the back of her leg held her flesh together.

There was a snap.

Virgil jumped back. The wolf charged wildly through the broken gate. It was a freight train breaking loose. Virgil dodged. He kept the sword down. The wolf spun quickly. A trail of spit seemed to hover while it turned as if in orbit. Virgil took a long swing with his sword to keep the wolf back. The wolf swatted it away. The wolf leapt forward. One arm extended, its claws pulled in. The impact knocked Virgil back. His heels left lines as he skidded. Dust trailed his feet.

Riley felt her fingers twitching. Her breaths were fast and shallow.

Behind the fence, Dove was a whirlwind of cloth and steel. The wolves twisted to keep up with her. They looked like dogs chasing nonexistent tails, their teeth snapping and their claws out. They were looking for blood. Her giddy laugh bounced between them. She shot one quick strike at a wolf as it turned toward her. There was a sharp howl of pain. She bounced away as the wolf's knee gave out. It tried to follow her before dropping to the ground.

Far in the distance, at the very edge of her sight, Riley could just make out the black cloaks of Sister Carolyn and the unknown brother. They seemed to have their arms and hands extended. A few other wolves were tucked behind the door of the shed or hidden within the leftover vegetation. A couple even knelt low to the ground, their hands flat on the grass and dirt, their heads pointed toward the conflict in front of them, as though ready to spring at any moment. Riley couldn't hear her fellow guardians from here. She imagined they were telling the wolves to remain calm, that nothing worse needs to happen.

A guttural scream rattled Riley's skull.

Virgil staggered forward. His leg dragged. His cloak was wide open. One hand gripped his sword while the other braced his left hip. Left leg. Like hers. Shredded cloth led to where his hand covered the wound. He huffed through gritted teeth.

The wolf stalked toward Virgil. Claws extended from hands held out front, blood dripping from nails, eyes burning, exposed upper fangs almost crossing those sticking up from the bottom of its jaw. As it inhaled its nostrils widened, whiskers and fur fluttered when it exhaled.

Virgil pointed his sword out as he stepped. He rotated his back to Riley. His left leg slid against the dirt road. The wolf didn't advance. It followed him with its glowing eyes.

It had been too dark for her to see then, that other night. A thick wetness had soaked into the soft ceiling cover. She would be able to see it now, every drop of deep crimson that fell from her wounds as she hung helplessly from the strap holding her to the passenger seat. Of course, if she had been then as she was now, she might have been able to see the accident coming. Perhaps she'd have seen the wolf in their path. She'd definitely have been able to heal faster at least. Maybe she could have saved Remy's life. She could have at least tried, instead of having to be pulled out while he was left to die.

Riley watched as Virgil rotated around. The wolf had its back to her. She popped up from her position in the trees. The wind rushed past her ears as she darted toward the dirt road leading to the clearing beyond the fence. She felt the cloak flutter lightly behind her. She wouldn't be as hidden as possible. She'd be a ghost, at least for a moment. Riley leapt just as the wolf turned. She smashed her foot against its skull. Her bones stung from the impact. It was like kicking a concrete wall. She landed softly, the fingertips of one gloved hand tapping the dirt. Her left foot stung but didn't hurt. If there had been any damage from her kick, it was already healed. Virgil hobbled several feet opposite of the wolf. He moved to a flanking position. The wolf took a moment to gather itself. It eyed them as it stepped away.

The wolf's red eyes darted between the two of them. Virgil slumped on his wounded leg while Riley remained low, fingertips pressing the ground, readied on the balls of her feet. She felt the same spring in her legs as she did on the mat. The wolf towered over her. What did it see when it looked down at her? She'd been told that they saw through smell. That's why the cloaks, gloves, pants, and shoes were all treated before they went out at night. That's why the Prior, the leader, anointed himself before engagement. The wolf's eyes lingered over her for a moment. It must have known she was there. Its lips curled, exposing the deep yellow roots of its four large fangs. Claws covered the tops of hands large enough to overlap themselves around her arm. Virgil's blood dripped from two of its nails. She saw the individual strands of hair that stretched up and into spikes. The points were more like sloppier clumps of dirt and grease than the armor of a fearsome warrior. The claws made it fierce, as did the pairs of sharp fangs, the blood-red eyes, and the muscles she could see tensing through ripples in those sloppy clumps.

Its fur shook as it pushed forward. She saw the tension in its shoulders and torso. She saw the muscles flex, and the power it took to lift its heavy arms. She saw its attack coming, pulling back before a long downward arc.

There was an opening.

Her knuckles smacked against the beast's chest. It felt as though her fingers would break.

The wolf crumpled inward. Its breath was a gust of stale wind. There was a whine as it tried to inhale. It staggered back a couple of steps, one massive hand covering the spot between the ribs and the upper abdomen. It was exactly where she'd wanted to hit. She bolted to the side, placing herself between the wolf and Virgil.

"Back," she said, placing one hand behind her. She glanced over her shoulder. Virgil still clutched where his left hip had been caught by the wolf's strike. "Back," she repeated, motioning for him to get behind her as she rotated to place the recovering wolf's back to the fence.

The wolf's shoulders lifted several feet as it drew in a deep breath. It curled its long claws low and in front of itself. The collection of ten razors looked like the maw of some predator fish deeper in the water than light could travel. The wolf's neck stretched forward. Its head tilted back as it took a long sniff of the air. It narrowed its eyes, squinting at her.

Its growls seemed to form words. "There," she thought she heard it say. The sides of its mouth curled up. It sniffed once more. It growled and recoiled slightly. Its gaze skipped over her, and it looked across the road. She was invisible.

Riley took another step back, hand still reaching toward where Virgil remained behind her. Her fingertips brushed his cloak.

"Go," she whispered instinctively.

"No more," he replied.

She glanced back. "You're hurt," she whispered over her shoulder.

There was a sharp growl ahead. Riley turned to see the wolf's eyes trained on her, narrowed and pained as though looking directly into the sun. Spit extended as it opened its mouth wide, a low roar rumbling from the back of its throat.

"Go," she yelled as the wolf braced to pounce.

A sharp howl cut through the air. It cut off. A cheery laugh replaced it. The wolf spun in place.

Dove was on one knee in the clearing beyond the fence. One arm was extended as though holding up the wolf that shook and twitched over her. Riley stared at where the blade pierced underneath the wolf's jaw. Dove giggled as she yanked the blade across and out. The wolf seemed to hover there, quivering. It almost enfolded her. Blood rained down. She stood and stepped away as the wolf's body gave out. An eye for an eye.

Riley could see two other wolves in the clearing several feet away from where Dove stood over the collapsed wolf. She turned her back on them, facing the spiked wolf seething back at her from the road beyond the face. Dove ran her tongue along the flat side of the bloodied blade. Another body lay in the grass several feet away. A long gash cut across its belly, saturating the ground with dark intestinal blood. The body was naked. The body was human.

"Such a waste," Virgil said from over Riley's shoulder. The wolf glanced toward her.

The wolf hesitated a moment as though deciding whom to attack.

Beyond the fence, Dove turned her attention to the two remaining wolves that lingered far from her. They looked almost afraid.

"This one is strong," Virgil said. "He would be good for our stock."

The wolf snorted loudly before turning back. Dust kicked up as it sprang toward the broken gate separating the road from the clearing, separating itself from Dove. In the clearing, Riley could see two bodies. The second bore a deep slash across its throat. It was also human.

"Death lifts their curse," Riley heard from behind her. "Doesn't mean they are forgiven."

The other two wolves seemed immediately encouraged as the other joined their group. The spiked one was clearly the largest. Blood shot out as Dove retracted her blade. She jumped away as the largest charged, she spun once more out of reach.

"I tried to talk to him," Virgil said through calming breaths.

Riley watched as Dove continued to evade her three attackers. She was an older kid toying with the younger ones on the playground, a mosquito dodging clapping hands.

"I said we were only interested in finding out who was behind the murders."

Dove's laugh rode on the breeze.

"You saw how he reacted. There is no reasoning with savages."

Dove ducked as the striped one took a wide swipe. She bounced over the grass. She was playing with them.

"They are not people," Virgil continued. "They're monsters."

"You're hurt," Riley said, turning away from Dove and toward Virgil. Blood streaked from his hip to his knee.

"Doesn't matter," he replied. The lines in his face were clean cracks in stone.

"You're exposed," she said.

"That's my purpose." Virgil tapped the front of his hood. "I am the light, so that others may work in the dark."

There was a quick yelp as Dove landed a short stab on one of the remaining wolves before once again bouncing out of their reach. She'd pulled them farther into the grass of the clearing, near the rocks and bushes where the wolves had first emerged and far from where the two bodies lay still on the ground. Their bare flesh was a sharp contrast from the dark fur they'd been covered with.

"And what are we?"

In the far distance she could see where the others, Sister Carolyn and the unnamed brother, continued to hold other wolves within the storage shed which looked so deteriorated that it could fall over at any moment.

"You told me that they are predators," she said, glancing back to where Virgil watched his prized pupil at work. The top of her head barely reached his shoulder. "And that we are guardians."

Virgil took a long breath. He closed his eyes. He flinched, the lines at the sides of his face squeezed.

"They've been warned," Riley said. "They've been punished."

"Sister Sapphira," Virgil said, exhaling. "You're right."

He blinked his eyes open. The pupils immediately adjusted. He lifted his hand from the wound. He shook the blood from his palm.

"Been a long time," he said quietly, as though to himself. "A long time."

Virgil looked over her. Riley kept her focus on him. She heard the sounds of heavy breath and struggle, rushed footsteps, wild swings through air, fluttering cloth, and laughter. Virgil took a deep breath. "Sister!" he yelled so loudly that Riley started for a moment. "Withdraw!"

He put the hand over the wound once more, slumping down as though every bit of weight and pain that he'd been holding off had suddenly rushed into his body. "Come, Sister Sapphira," he said. His leg dragged as he turned, but less so than before, "We've said all we can, tonight." Virgil limped forward, the dirt crunched under his steps.

Riley retreated slowly. The fence leaned outward, lines of barbed wire sagging at the top. The chain hung from one side of the fence, one link clearly ripped open. The seat to a broken chair was nearly buried in the dirt right in front of the fence. Dove was a blur across the field. Three wolves bounded after her in awkward, unbalanced ways. Far in the distance was the overgrown grass and sparse bushes of the clearing, the building near the back end. She could just make out the figures starting to sneak out from behind the rusted door, its green paint faded and cracked from age and sun. The others had already withdrawn. Then closer, where grass replaced dirt, the two bloodstained bodies lay still, the edges of grass blades beneath them.

Riley kept her head lowered as she walked away. She focused on the roots of the first set of trees after the tall grass at the edge of the dirt road. Virgil was several steps ahead. She followed him back into the forest.

Virgil grunted as he took another short step on his injured leg.

Riley peeked over her shoulder. It felt like

they'd been walking only a few minutes, yet the clearing was long gone behind them. Not a trace of the wolves since they'd left. Not a trace of Dove either, nor Carolyn or their brother. Just the two of them, walking far slower than she had expected they would.

Virgil grunted once more.

"The deep ones don't heal as quickly as they used to," he said, breathing out heavily.

He took a moment to shake his head. He turned to her. A calm had come over his face. The cracks were as deep as ever, yet smoothed. They seemed more designed than grown at random. He nodded as she stepped even to him.

"Even we get older, Riley. We can't . . . do the things we used to." His view drifted up to the branches overhead. The leaves flapping in the wind were so constant they were little more than white noise in her ears, like the hum of a television behind the commotion on-screen. The corners of his mouth ticked up. "Never thought I'd last this long," he said. He took a deep breath, exhaled it slowly. "Thought the corruption would have taken me long, long ago."

Riley looked back the way they'd come. Still no sign of any pursuit, no wolves, no others, nothing. "How long?" she asked.

"Forever," he replied. "All my life."

"How old were you when you took the sacrament?"

He turned his focus to her. His eyes were faded almost to white. She knew he couldn't see hers through the shadow which remained over them, the same darkness which allowed her to see his in the night.

"I don't even remember," he said after a quiet moment. "Long enough that the corruption has become my own."

Riley tilted her head at this.

"We are bound now, you and I," he said.

She blinked her gaze away. "By the blood."

"No," he dismissed, "by life. You saved me

tonight, just as I once saved you." There was a series of three pops. Riley looked over to see Virgil stretching his neck to the side, another three pops followed. "Perhaps this will not be the last time."

"Perhaps," she replied.

He laughed, low and quick.

"One day, Riley, if you're very lucky, you'll get to feel this way." He nodded. "Someday. Long after my time is done."

Virgil turned, still nodding. He took a step with his injured leg, a longer step than before.

"After I earn my chance to die."

# CHAPTER 8

THE CROWD OVERWHELMED THE CONCRETE PATHS of the plaza. The car slowed as it passed those parked at the side of the road. Pedestrians darted across to join the crowd pressing toward the numerous television crews who'd set up large antennae for remote broadcasts.

It seemed to Nate that the entire town was now concentrated at that one point. He imagined every shop, home, and office completely empty. Then he lowered his head as a group of four people crossed the street just in front of his mom's truck. The hoodie and sunglasses might have made him look like the suspect from every cop movie made in the last twenty years, but at least he looked human. He kept his head down as his mother flipped on the turn signal and waited for the cars in the museum lot to finally exit after seeing that all the spots were taken. The car behind followed them in closely, backing off only once Nate's mother started a U-turn to pull up to the front of the stairs. He kept his face toward the floor while several other cars waited for the turn to complete.

Shayera stood at the curb. A black leather jacket covered her red tank top.

"Well," Nate's mother said as she pulled to a stop, other cars already cramming around her to pass. "Good luck, I suppose." She unlocked the doors.

"Yeah," he said. He could barely look at her.

She glanced at the cars squeezed tightly into the small lot with barely inches between them. "I can try to find a place to park," she said, "I can come—"

"No."

144

Shayera pulled the door open before Nate could. He turned his back to his mother as he exited and held the hood in place while climbing out of the car.

"All right then," his mother replied.

Onlookers lined the museum steps. They stared across the lot and into the packed center of the plaza. New cars pushed others from the parking lot on the slim chance that one of the vehicles leaving had left an open space that none of the many, many others in front of it had noticed. Nate noticed Canadian license plates. Those farther south would take a while longer to arrive, probably longer than anyone hoped the story would last.

Shayera bent to look into Nate's mother's truck. "Mrs. Wallace," she said, before suddenly lowering her head as though addressing royalty.

"Shayera," his mother replied, "you're looking well."

"Thank you, High—Mrs. Wallace."

Nate turned from where Shayera remained uncomfortably bent toward the open door. He rolled his eyes. A clear path wound through the people clustered along the stairs up to the museum.

"I hope you will speak well of my son," Nate heard his mother say from within the car.

"Of . . . of course, High—Mrs. Wallace."

"Samantha," his mother said.

"Of course."

A couple descended the stairs, stretching and tiptoeing to see over the cars and into the center of the plaza. Their view shifted to the curb in front of them. Nate lowered his head and twisted away before they could see him. Or so he hoped.

"Stand up, Shayera," Nate's mom added. The cars behind her were growing impatient.

"Ye-yes," Shayera said.

Shayera straightened up. She pushed her shoulders back as even as her head remained slightly turned, avoiding eye contact.

"One other favor I need from you right now," his mother said.

"Yes?"

"Close the door. We're holding up traffic."

"Ye-yes. Of course, High—Mrs.—Samantha Wallace."

Shayera slammed the door shut. She turned in a sudden, jarring motion, seeming to twitch as she faced Nate at the foot of the staircase.

"If you like her so much, you can have her," he remarked. He caught his mother's eye through the window as she pulled away. She gave a wink.

"She's your mother," Shayera said, her confidence restored once more. "You should appreciate that."

"Get to know her like I do. I think your impression will change."

"And I don't think you want to make another person angry with you right now," Shayera replied sternly. "Especially when that person may be the only ally you have left."

"Can't say I'm not consistent."

Nate kept his head down and hands tucked into the pouch pocket at the front of his hoodie as they walked. The weather wasn't quite right for such a thick sweater, but standing out as being overdressed was preferable to standing out for another possible reason.

"Already pissed off everyone else," he said, "why not make it a clean sweep?"

"Don't say that," Shayera replied as they reached the first landing.

Nate waited to speak until they passed a group of people staring into the plaza. "So," he said, still quietly enough that he hoped only she could hear him. "I heard last night that werewolves are responsible for hundreds of murders all over the country."

Shayera said nothing as she moved behind him to fit through a narrow gap in the crowd on the second landing.

"Possibly thousands," he continued, "tens of thousands, over several decades."

"Don't," Shayera replied as they approached parents with a small child.

"I even heard that werewolves are the reason

every American should have a gun in their house. Several guns, all of them automatics, kept loaded and with the safeties off."

They reached the last set of stairs.

"Because you never know."

There was an audible sigh.

"I also heard that werewolves faked the moon landing."

Nate heard the footsteps behind him stop as he climbed the last stair. He turned back to look at where Shayera stared at him, lower than usual. She shook her head. "Don't," she said again. He looked over her and into the crowd beyond.

Through the gaps in the park trees, he saw a dense crowd near where the four paths met. A line of metal fences and police officers closed off the very center of the plaza. Television cameras, each filming a separate report, rimmed the fountain in the center of the park, the water having been turned off to keep the ambient noise down. There were signs among some in the crowd, white posters, some with words and some with pictures. Nate couldn't tell what any of them were, but he doubted they were good. The crowd spilled out unevenly throughout the symmetrical design. It was the new chaos.

"Did you see the news?" he asked. "I already did."

She stepped up to join him on the last step, turning to look over the crowd as he did.

The congestion lessened at the outer edges of the plaza until reaching the sidewalks where pedestrians looked over the bushes and circled around for a better view. The cars continued to crawl by. The few neighboring streets he could see were lined with cars along every curb. The only people were those coming to join the rest of the crowd.

"Biggest party of the year," Nate remarked. "A shame the guest of honor can't come."

"No one else thinks this is funny," Shayera snapped.

"That's because no one else is heading to the gallows."

Wispy clouds hung low in the sky as darker ones

loomed over the outskirts of the town. It was the tail end of summer. Autumn would be coming soon. Then the long winter. Dark and cold.

"The world is changing," Nate said.

"Always is," Shayera answered, "and yet nothing is different."

He squinted to see a group of people pacing down the sidewalk across the museum parking lot. A man flanked by two small children held a placard against his shoulder like a rifle. GOD HATES MONSTERS read the sign.

"All right," Shayera finally said. Nate followed her turn toward the concrete building face. Shayera strode ahead. "We shouldn't keep them waiting."

"Yeah," Nate replied, moving behind her. "Or I might be in trouble." A few exhibit posters remained on the long columns advertising special tours for students on summer vacation. "At least the crowd should bring the museum a few extra visitors."

"Extra visitors is the last thing any of us need."

Ulrich stood several steps in front of the tapestry over the rear wall, surrounded by others whom Nate vaguely recognized from his previous appearances at much smaller Council meetings. "We just want to understand what happened, that's all," Ulrich said, gesturing for Nate to step toward the middle of the room, in view of everyone gathered in the last gallery of the museum.

Across from Ulrich, as always, was Maier. A step behind Maier was Zarker, posing as a bearded man who fidgeted comfortably at the sleeves of a frumpy sweater. There were Clarkson and Wald, along with dozens of people he didn't recognize. Shayera remained at Nate's side in front of the opening between the main chamber and the hallway.

"Please," Ulrich said calmly, "tell us your story."

Nate took a step forward. "My story," Nate said, looking at the crowd around him. He thought of the people in the plaza outside packed around an almost empty center to stare at cameras, reporters, and police with the fountain in the middle. There were fewer in here, in a smaller space, and with the center removed, but they stared nonetheless.

"My story," he said again. In the cleared center he could see the pattern on the gray stone in the floor. Six pointed shafts of dark gray over light branched from a common origin in the middle. He looked around the room, reading the faces: Maier's stern expression, Clarkson's concern, Wald's look of understanding, Ulrich's studied indifference, Zarker's sneer. He saw that Shayera had turned away, as though unable to watch. It was the first time Nate could remember that she hadn't been standing next to Ulrich. Instead she remained a step behind his side, like one of Joe Pesci's escorts in *Goodfellas*, the ones who kill him.

"Go on, son," Ulrich said, "we're listening."

Maier crossed his hands in front of him. He raised his chin.

He'd told Nate yesterday that there had been a time when wolves—Fenrei—were free. A time when his kind didn't need to live in fear of discovery or hatred or slaughter. It was only when they chose to give up that right, when the others—other people—came into their territory that the danger started. Perhaps, Maier had said, if they had continued to live openly, then today, more than two centuries later, his people would be accepted in society along-side other once-hated and vilified groups.

"Don't worry," Ulrich urged. "We want to hear everything you wish to tell."

Maier was right, the old ways wouldn't work any-more. After yesterday, there was no way they could. It was foolish to try. Ulrich had to know that too. There was no way he couldn't.

The word "scapegoat" rang through Nate's mind. Probably the best way to shield the rest of them would be to offer one as the lone culprit. A sacrifice to be targeted, hated, seized, experimented on, while the rest of them waited for the uproar to die down and then continued in secrecy, the way they had for years. It was the closest thing they could get to the old ways. And he was the ideal sacrifice.

Nate shook his head. "You already know my story," he said at last. "You saw it all on the news last night." He waved a hand in the direction of the museum entrance. "I viciously attacked a helpless waiter. I chased him down a crowded street in the middle of the day in front of dozens of people in malicious violation of the conditions of our Code."

He surveyed the faces he could see in the crowd. Anger, annoyance, frustration, distress, and intense glares surrounded him. He settled back on Ulrich.

"We of the blood shall never harm a human," Nate recited. "Yet you all saw me do just that." Ulrich took a deep breath which he released slowly. "None but those of the blood shall know we exist. Yet, they all saw me. In fact," Nate threw his hands up in fake revelation, "I'm famous. I guess that's three rules I've broken."

Ulrich flexed his jaw.

"By now the whole world knows my story." Nate let his hands drop back to his sides. He saw Ulrich stare at him, his expression more of disappointment than anger. Nate looked away. He wanted to take a step back into the rest of the crowd but couldn't, not after such a speech.

Ulrich shook his head.

"I had such high hopes for you," he said. "The full-blooded offspring of the Wallace and Chavis lines. So much potential." He sighed. "Such a waste."

"High hopes," Nate repeated, "yet you haven't believed me from the start."

There was a flash of rage in Ulrich's expression before he settled again on sadness, almost pity.

"I told you for two months about how the Order intentionally provoked me into changing that night of the incident." He motioned toward Clarkson and Zarker, "I told you just a few days ago that Dove tried to goad me into attacking them," he motioned toward Shayera a step behind him, "and you had me thrown out of this chamber." Nate shook his head in disbelief. "So why should I think you'll listen to my story now? You have all the proof you need."

"We want to know what the cameras can't tell us," Ulrich said with a suspicious calm.

"What difference will it make?" Nate glanced to where Maier stood with his arms crossed, head lowered, and brow furrowed. "You didn't believe me when there weren't half a dozen videos, so why would you believe what I have to tell you now? How can I prove that this guy, John, or whatever his name is, threatened my mother and my friends? That he threatened every single person in this room right now before stabbing a friend of mine"—he threw his arms out for emphasis—"who has nothing to do with any of this, just to make me angry. Just to make me react the way I did. The same exact thing they've been pushing me to do since before I even knew that any of this," he waved his hand at the room around him, "even existed. Before I even knew what I am." He looked around at the rest of the crowd. Hostility greeted him. "And now I'm supposed to think that you just 'want to understand what happened'?"

Ulrich folded his arms across his chest.

"Yeah, right," Nate said. There were gasps among some in the crowd, discontented grumbles among others. "You didn't want to 'hear everything I wish to tell,'" he spouted in a mocking tone, "and you don't want to hear it now."

Ulrich opened his mouth as though about to speak.

"What you want is an easy excuse to blame me for everything that's happened since my very first night. What you want," he paused, remembering Maier's visit the day before, "is a scapegoat."

Ulrich nodded slowly. "You're right," he said. "I do want someone to blame this on." Sounds of shock reverberated through the crowd. "Someone to blame for yesterday and for these murders, and for everything that has happened to this community since the night you became a part of it." Red flashed through Ulrich's eyes. "And everyone in this room, and everyone outside of this room, wants the same thing." There was force in Ulrich's tone. "We don't just want it. We demand it."

Ulrich gestured outwardly as though addressing the entire world.

"I've been in touch with Councils from all over the world, and they are all demanding that the guilty party turn himself over or be turned over." His tone went quieter, calmer. "I've told them that any such thing would result in that person being taken away, experimented on, dissected, tortured." His eyes came up to meet Nate's. "They said that if I didn't turn you over, then they would. Although they also offered a simpler, more humane option," he said flatly. "Execution."

Whispers in the crowd.

Ulrich continued. "You have brought nothing but pain to this community from the moment you joined us. I personally attempted to bring you in, to teach you to control your gifts, to mold you into a position fit for your lineage. Instead, you have compromised our most sacred practices and exposed our greatest secret to the entire world." A sneer twitched on Ulrich's face. "You aren't a scapegoat. A scapegoat carries the sins of others into the wilderness." He shook his head. "You are a sacrifice."

"And what proof do we have that this sacrifice will be enough?" Nate snapped his vision to Maier as the older man spoke up from the crowd. "The populace knows we exist. They know there is more than one of us in the world. Sacrificing just one of our kind will do nothing to quell their bloodlust. It may, in fact, only increase their desire to see our kind exterminated." Maier raised his chin to look across at Ulrich. "What happens then? More of these sacrifices? How will we decide who to present for public execution? How many will be acceptable?"

There were sparse sounds of agreement from the crowd.

"The Order never troubled us before this boy came into our ranks," Ulrich countered.

"The Order isn't our concern, High Councilor," Maier responded. "Not any more. Times have changed. We are faced with a frightened populace, which knows nothing about the honor binding our kind to theirs. They only know that we are not like them and are, thus, dangerous."

"A revelation which never would have happened if it weren't for the rash, undisciplined actions of—"

"But it did happen!" Nate snapped. The interruption caused disapproval in the crowd. "And no amount of promises or threats or punishments is going to change that." He grew quieter. "If the last several months have taught me anything, it's that nothing we will ever do can change what has already happened."

"The Order has always trusted us to handle our own discipline," Ulrich said, as though his even tone would calm the crowd. "Doing so now would demonstrate that we remain as committed to our obligation as ever before. We have always been partners in this secret."

"Not anymore," Nate interrupted again.

"Only according to you, one whose lack of discipline has compromised everything that our kind had worked for two hundred years to sustain."

"Two hundred years that could have been spent living freely and as equals," Maier opined.

"Two hundred years of trust and peace," Ulrich continued. "Two hundred years during which this community has been able to grow in both size and influence. To establish a shelter for those of our kind," his eyes drifted to Nate, "even when they are ignorant or in denial of who they truly are."

Nate's anger rose as the stares returned to him.

"Yes," Maier said before Nate could find his words. "There has always been trust between this Council and the Order. As per the conditions of the Accord, they have always known our identities." Maier gestured toward Nate, "This would give credence to Nathaniel's claim that his family and those he cares for have been threatened by this man prior to his actions."

Nate nodded.

Ulrich brushed one hand in dismissal. "Where's the proof of this?"

Nate couldn't help but wonder why neither Craig nor Tony had come forward with their stories of what happened that day. Probably out of fear. Craig's house had already been stormed once. He'd also been stabbed. And only after that did he learn that his friend was a monster.

Maier looked around the room as though appealing to the gathered crowd. "The Order has already demonstrated a willingness to violate the conditions of the Accord by forcing Nathaniel into a change he was unaware of and unprepared for."

"According to his account," Ulrich muttered.

"They tried to kill me!" Nate yelled. "They almost killed Riley."

"No," Ulrich said, "they wouldn't dare kill her."

"What does—"

"High Councilor," Maier said as he took a step from his place in the circle. He nodded to Nate before continuing. "The Order has further broken our trust by framing one of our kind for the murder of Dawn Musgrave and those of Roderick and Melanie Bailey, as well as their sons. It broke our trust by provoking a . . ."—he looked at Ulrich as he motioned to Nate—"novice in our ranks into attacking what I'm sure we can all understand was a blackrobe posing as a waiter. And it was broken last night when Father Vigilius himself marched into a settlement without cause, in order to assault and slaughter our kind."

A tremor ran through the crowd.

Ulrich tilted his head and narrowed his eyes at Maier. "Is this true?"

"Yes, High Councilor," Zarker said as he bowed away. One hand wiped at his baggy pants leg. "Five of them came during the night. I spoke to the black-robe leader myself." His voice was surprisingly high as a man, far from the snarled, guttural sounds he normally made. "He said that they would no longer tolerate our kind." He picked at the sleeve of his shirt, eyes still lowered. "He said that we'd tainted the land for too long, and that he was the point of the spear that would remove us from creation." His eyes closed. He stopped picking at his clothes. His hand still shook. "He said he was there to take my family away, just as we had taken away his." Zarker shook his head as though in pain. "That's when I attacked."

"So you attacked them?" Ulrich asked.

"They killed Clay and Hercules while I was distracted by Vigilius and another—a small one who I didn't recognize. They were covered and quick."

"You were the aggressor," Ulrich prompted.

"They threatened my family just as they threatened Nathaniel's. Their leader said they would wipe our kind from the planet. They would have killed more of my people, Francis and Fabian, if I hadn't stopped them."

Maier leaned toward Zarker back in the circle. "Tell them who the murderer was."

Zarker's nostrils flared. "Dove."

Nate heard the laughter rattle in his head. He imagined the pointed fingers in the dark, the mimicked gunshot with an explosion of fire and metal before the pop of the tire, the crash, and the shattering glass. Dove had been there every time. Every time.

"Surely this action proves the Order's intentions," Maier exclaimed from his place one step in front of the circle. Several around him nodded at this. "The Prior and his lieutenant personally moved upon a peaceful, independent settlement just to threaten and murder its occupants." The room filled with sounds of both concession and disagreement. "The Order has declared war upon us."

"A war started only after one of our kind exposed himself to the entire world," Ulrich countered. His thin finger pointed directly at Nate, snapping him from the memories of laughter, gunfire, and shredding metal. "There was peace before his arrival. How do we know that he hasn't provoked these actions himself?"

"Because I say so."

There was a shocked gasp.

"Who is—"

People parted from between the chamber and the hall. Silence followed Nate's mother as she moved toward the open middle. The entire crowd seemed to bow their heads as one. Nate couldn't help feeling a slight relief at the sound of her voice.

"High Councilor Ulrich," she said in a more regal tone than Nate was familiar with, as though she were a character from a British prestige drama. "If someone is to be blamed for my son's actions, let it be me."

Even Ulrich angled slightly downward as he spoke. "I . . . I wouldn't dare to blame—"

"You should," Nate's mother answered with slightly less elevation than before. "If I had told my son about his gifts before, if I had fulfilled my duties as his guardian and teacher . . . " Those gathered remained bowed as she spoke. " . . . offered him a true Feral Right, then perhaps these tragedies could have . . . " She glanced to Nate a few steps away from her. An annoyed look came over her face. "Okay, you can look at me now. I'm not the damn sun," she said.

Nate tried not to laugh as every head rose around him. His mother placed her hand on his shoulder. "You okay?" she asked quietly.

Nate nodded, the resentment of the last few days lessening.

"You know that just because you heard me curse here doesn't mean that it's okay for—"

Nate nodded again.

She patted his shoulder, turning back to address the crowd.

"I withdrew my family and kept my son in the dark," she said. "I hoped that by moving away we'd be left alone." She paused to look over the ocean of wide stares in her direction. "I was wrong. If anyone should be held responsible for all that's happened, it should be me."

Ulrich straightened himself before speaking. "This council has no interest in assigning blame—"

"That's not what it sounded like when I came in here. In fact, there was so much chatter going on that I was able to walk right through the door without anyone even noticing. Lucky I wasn't someone more malicious."

"With all due respect, High Councilor Wallace," Ulrich replied, "your husband created a legacy of peaceful coexistence. His relationship with Father Pius is one that I strove to emulate with Father Innocent and hoped to continue with Father Vigilius until this recent . . . ugliness."

Nate stifled a laugh.

"Your husband," Ulrich continued, "your son's father, dedicated his life to preserving this community from threats, including those which rise within our ranks. He never would have tolerated anyone endangering our place in this town or our position among human society."

"And where did that get him?" Maier snapped.

"Disgraceful," muttered someone in the crowd.

"High Councilor," Ulrich continued, "imagine you are in my position, as you had been years ago. A new member of our community has emerged and with him has come a string of violent incidents culminating in that member exposing our kind in front of the entire world. What would you do in that case?"

The entire crowd stared as Nate's mother crossed her arms and locked her jaw at Ulrich.

"Remove the fact that he is your son and tell us, honestly, what would your action be."

"I can't," she said. "I tried removing him from the rest of you. Here we are."

"Yes," Ulrich said, "you removed him from his kind, yet you allowed him to develop a friendship with theirs."

The stares continued, confusion and hints of disgust creeping into several of the faces around the room. Nate's mother scratched one hand across her forearm so roughly it should have bled. The sides of her nose pinched up, like they had in the hospital the morning Nate awoke after the incident.

"How do you explain this, High Councilor?" Ulrich prodded. "How are we to take your judgment as valid . . . "

Nate glanced over as his mother shook her head forcefully. Red tint leaked into her eyes. Her fingers twitched from adrenaline.

" . . . when you allow the only child of our fallen leader to pal around with the child of—"

"QUIET!"

His mother's voice was a piercing roar that shook the entire room. She stalked forward, through the open space between the dense rim of onlookers. Her breaths were seething rumbles as she walked directly up to Ulrich's face. The old man straightened up but didn't back away.

"Don't you dare lecture me," she growled.

Nate leaned in, an attempt to see over his mother's shoulder.

"Don't you dare instruct me on how to raise or

protect *my* son." Her words were angry, driven, but controlled. She snapped her view back and forth across those standing around Ulrich. "None of you have any right to—"

"Mom?" Nate said. His own voice rang in his ears like that of a child.

She didn't turn. She stood motionless for a moment before her shoulders slumped. She appeared to shrink before him. Murmurs arose from the far reaches of the assembly.

"Father Pius," she said after what felt like hours of silence, "was Clarence McKnight. Riley's father."

Nate felt himself waver. A cold crept over him as the room began to spin. It seemed as though he was falling, even as he stood. There were noises around him, grunts and gasps and whispers and words he didn't hear. He wanted to drop to the floor, but he didn't. He wanted to speak, to ask questions, to make sure he'd heard what he thought he'd heard, but he couldn't.

They'd sat at the side of so-called Patrick Wallace

Creek watching the bubbles gather in the rapidly moving water before making a promise that may have never happened, but it became real. They'd hopped fences in people's backyards to wander through the forest when told not to. They'd sat on the couch in front of the open door of his bedroom, shushing each other for even the slightest utterance while watching countless films. He'd sat next to her hospital bed while she slept with her leg suspended in a thick cast and felt himself breaking inside from the promise they may have never made.

His head shook with a nervous tick as his mind raced from memories to questions: Did she know about her father? When had she learned about him? Had she known about Nate? How long? His mind flooded. If Father Vigilius knew everything about him, how couldn't she? What about the crash? Had she known then? Why had they targeted her? Had it been staged? Had she been at the train tracks that night? He flashed through every moment they'd shared together, every story they'd told, every single second he'd spent in her company. Were they all a lie?

"Why," he said under the noise that suddenly filled the room around him. "Why didn't you tell me?"

His mother continued arguing with Ulrich as Maier joined and others watched with their heads swiveling as though observing a tennis match.

"Why didn't you tell me!" he yelled.

Silence. His mother bolted to attention before slowly falling. She still didn't turn. Heat shot through his veins.

"Look at me!"

She shook as her eyes rose to meet his. Water danced over them.

"You lied to me about yourself," Nate said. His eyes flashed to Maier and back to his mother. "You lied to me about Dad. You lied to me about who I am, and you lied to me about Riley."

"I didn't lie," she muttered, "I just didn't tell you." Her gaze dropped to avoid him.

Fire licked at the back of his throat. "Didn't tell me?" he said, unable to believe her words. Not now. "Didn't *tell me?*"

She flinched as though about to be struck.

He looked over the rest of the room. Most stood with their eyes cast down. Ulrich shook his head as though in condemnation. Zarker twitched uncomfortably. Maier glanced up, looking solemn.

"Has anything you've ever actually told me been the truth?" Nate said slowly. "Or has everything always been a lie?" He paused for a moment before speaking again. "Oh wait," he said, a sudden lightness to his tone, "how could you answer that without telling yet another lie? It's no wonder no one here believes me, I've never in my entire life *heard* the truth!"

He watched as his mother tried to shrink away. Those around her did the same, all of them with their heads down and unable to speak or move. They were cowards.

"Enough," he said. He felt a slight well at the

corner of one eye. "Enough with all of you. All of your lies."

He turned. The crowd parted before him.

"Don't," his mother whispered.

They stared as he started away.

"Don't leave." A hand clasped his arm. Nate turned to see Shayera standing behind him. Her hand remained tight around his arm. She shook her head.

"Don't touch me," he growled.

Shayera pushed her shoulders back. She looked fearful but firm.

"Let me go," he said.

"I can't," she said, tightening her grip.

"Nathaniel." His mother looked like she was about to shatter.

He shoved Shayera back with his free arm. She lost her grip. The crowd gasped as she slid across the floor. He turned away.

There were footsteps and yells. He ignored them. The world fell into silence. He walked through the hallway to the gallery entrance. He passed the little drawers that contained every birth, death, marriage, name change, deed, every document of every person in the room behind him. Drawers that contained every secret. So many secrets. Too many of them. Secrets, lies, all of it. That time was gone. The era of lies had passed. They wouldn't work any longer.

It was time for the truth.

# CHAPTER 9

**S**HE'D PUSHED THE PIECES OF HER CAST TO ONE side of the bed. They were close enough that they'd be available quickly if needed and far enough away that they felt separate from everything else. They were from a period of her life that had ended as quickly as it had begun.

Riley kept her pillow folded over itself to prop her head up higher, angled to see the television on top of the shelf on the other side of her bedroom. Her left knee was bent, foot flat on the bed. She flexed the leg a couple of times, saw how the muscle bulged under the pale skin. Two small marks remained where a pair of screws had been briefly planted to set the bone in her thigh. She reached to feel the scar on the back of her leg, about half an inch wide and five, six, maybe seven inches long.

" . . . Even as more stories come in every day. Local police remain reluctant to release any further information on the murders of the Bailey Family, Dawn Musgrave, or issue a definitive statement on whether these incidents are related." The woman on the television pushed the hair out of her eyes.

Riley stopped tracing her scar. She raised her right hand from the bed. She closed her hand and saw how the muscles reacted. That's where the blade would go, over the right forearm. Did that mean all of her brothers and sisters in the Order were right-handed as well, or was it tradition, like the Pledge of Allegiance or swearing in at court? The metal cover would prevent her from accidentally piercing her own hand, but it would also make it impossible to flatten. Handstands would have to be done on a fist. She'd probably get used to it pretty quick. It didn't take too long to become at least accustomed to walking on the crutches, although it took much less time to readjust to walking without them.

" . . . understand that no one has come forth with the identity of the boy in the video," said the man in the pinstripe suit seated in front of a computer-generated image of the New York skyline, as though being in the big city made their stories more accurate.

"Receiving names hasn't been the problem, Jack," the woman in front of the plaza fountain replied after a moment of delay. "In fact, police tell us their operators have received several tips as to the identity of the young-man-turned-wolf in the video. Those names include"— she looked down at a notepad in her hand—"several local residents, many of them female, David Naughton, who of course starred in *An American Werewolf in London*, Michael J. Fox, Lon Chaney Jr., Jacob Black, and quote: The chick from the *Underworld* movies, although I believe her character was a vampire."

"Sounds like quite a search."

"Ummm . . . " The woman in front of the fountain blinked a few times. "I suppose you could say that."

"Idiot," Riley remarked. She again pictured where the blade would emerge from under her sleeve. Did it ever get caught in the sleeve? The gloves were also treated, but not the blade, so wouldn't the wolves smell the metal once it stuck out? Of course, by the time you're in range to use the blade, you better be quick enough to strike before the wolf can.

She hadn't yet even been allowed to practice with the blade. She had to build up to that; blunt weapons, then edged ones, and then the wrist blade. The blade had to be earned. Some never made it that far or simply preferred a sword, a dagger, or even one of the antique pistols contained in the weapons cabinet across from the line of portraits which greeted her on every trip to her new physical therapy. Her new gymnastics team.

At first it seemed strange to her that an organization created to combat a creature so much stronger, faster, more savage than any other, would rely on antiquated weapons, especially when much more powerful ones were available. "In America," Nate told her, "anyone can have a concealed weapon." Now she did too. More than one, in fact. The difference was that her weapons weren't about dominance, or ease, or mass slaughter. It wasn't the need for protection that well-armed cowards prattle about. The Order's weapons were meant to make them equal with their charges. A wolf would never wield an AR-15, so why should those who are meant to guard them be any different? Such overkill wouldn't be protection. It would be terror.

It seemed to her that the real difference wasn't in the weapon but in the wielder. Even with their fancy automatics, so-called "sportsmen" would piss themselves at the sight of a spiked horror movie monster with the size and speed of a small car and the power of a big rig. Meanwhile, she'd stared directly at it, right in its glowing red eyes, armed with nothing but an odorless cloak and a swallow of its blood. She didn't blink. No, in that moment, she hit it so hard that it couldn't breathe. But if she'd been armed, she probably could have killed it. That was where the Canaanites and gun-wielding cowards were the same: those with the power to kill, killed. That's how a predator thought. Thus, those who wished to stand against a predator must be willing to do the same. If the wolves didn't have the power to kill, then she wouldn't need it either. But force needed to be met with equal force. There were laws about that.

A clamor sounded through her television. "—seems to be some sort of disturbance," said the woman as she leaned to the edge of the frame. "Mike, can we get a shot of this?"

There were cries from offscreen. The camera turned awkwardly. A trio of police in bright yellow vests clustered in one place. "Looks like someone jumped the barricade," the reporter said.

Shouts came from the person being held by the

police. The crowd behind the barricade pushed forward. The two sides seemed to be simultaneously holding back and being held back by one person in the middle. It looked to Riley like the scene in the restaurant before the transformation.

"—alone!" the voice yelled.

The camera zoomed into the backs of the police. A fourth officer came into the side of the screen. The camera focused on the person between the officers.

Riley bolted up on the bed. It was Nate.

"Just want to be left alone!" he yelled.

"Monsters!" yelled someone else in the crowd. "Murderers!" yelled another, or maybe the same, impossible to tell.

Riley leaned forward.

"No!" Nate yelled, whipping his head back even as the police kept him pushed against the barricade. "They want to live!"

"What's he saying?" asked a deep voice close by, the cameraman.

"He's talking about the wolves, I think."

"Don't want to be hunted!" Nate yelled. He bucked forward as someone shoved him from behind.

"Savages!" came another yell.

"Probably one of them!"

"Wolf lover!"

"No." Riley shook her head involuntarily. "No, no, no, no."

"Mike, do we have a clear shot of him?"

The camera zoomed in to where Nate stretched to see between the cops, jostling as members of the crowd pushed from behind. A white picket sign at the corner of the screen flashed the last four letters of the word FREAKS.

"—started this town!" Nate yelled. Another shout covered his. "—until now! Not once!"

The reporter spoke over the rest of the sound. "Can we tell if that's the same kid from the video?"

"—alone!" Nate yelled again.

The shaking spread through Riley's entire body.

"Please," she whispered, hands together in prayer, "please no. No, no. Not him."

"I know it!" Nate yelled. "I know—" his voice garbled into a growl.

"Oh God!" yelled the reporter.

Screams followed. Nate's face shook, or maybe the camera shook, or maybe Riley's head was shaking, or maybe all of them. He disappeared behind the police, an unfocused darkness emerging between them. A roar silenced everything else. The camera dropped to the ground.

Riley closed her eyes.

The reporter's voice again, cursing loudly. Then a shock of static. Then quiet. Then sounds of breathing and heavy steps, like those which echoed through the hall as she walked down the stairs during training.

Riley whispered, hands pressed together, "If you're there. Not him. Please. Anyone but him." Televised screams faded. She opened her eyes.

The image had turned sideways. There was a

bag on the ground, a metal thermos in front of it, a roll of duct tape a few feet away. At the top of the screen, unfocused in the background, was the police barricade. A massive furred foot came into view. The leg behind it tilted backward from toes with long nails emerging from the front. Riley jumped as a fang popped onto the screen. A set of sharpened teeth.

Loud breathing filled the air. The sound rolled into a long, low growl, a rumble, with high tones and pauses like syllables.

Riley felt the water drop on her chin. Her breath was caught and stuttered.

A snarled voice came through.

Riley screamed as the tears fell. She dropped forward. She buried her face in the blanket, fingers gripping into her scalp. Every part of her shook. She felt herself breaking.

The video played over and over and over but she'd turned off the sound.

Riley's mother carried a stack of framed pictures to the box on the dinner table. She placed them inside one by one, as careful as hasty.

Riley sat on the living room couch. The padding of her cast made her thigh itch.

"Roads will probably be too crowded to get out of here tonight," her mother said. "Should be clearer by tomorrow morning if the damn news vans and tourists aren't still clogging it up."

Riley's puffy eyes stung as she stared at the images on the screen of Nate, her best friend, the one who'd saved her from sadness after her dad died, who made her laugh when she thought nothing would ever be funny again, changed from the boy she knew into a beast, a monster, a terror. It was on every channel. Different angles. Some showed him change. Some showed the police aiming their pistols but not firing as the crowd fled in panic. Some showed him kneeling down, dark brown with patches of black needlelike hair covering his long back. Only one had the fang and set of teeth, the thin black fur that lined his pulled-back lip. It sounded like he was trying to say something, but no one knew what.

"Riley?"

She turned to see her mother placing another frame into the box.

"You need to start packing. It'll be slow but you can do it."

Riley turned back to the screen.

"I know that Nate would never hurt you or me but he's . . . you never know with them. And there are others who aren't . . . friends."

Riley turned toward her mother again. The last framed picture went into the box.

"Mom."

Her mother sighed as she broke eye contact.

"You know I can't leave with you."

Her mother walked out of the room. Riley stared

at the wall she disappeared behind until she reappeared, arms full of clothes.

"I can't."

"Have you taken the sacrament?" Riley's mother asked, not looking up from where she was stuffing the clothes into the gaps in the box.

"Yes."

Her mother sighed deeply. Her eyes closed and shoulders slumped.

"It's what Dad would have wanted."

Her mother locked into her eyes. "It's also what killed him. Did they tell you that?"

Riley saw her mother's bewilderment and frustration.

"Did they tell you what that stuff does?"

"It healed me."

"Sure for now, but once it gets into your system, once you're too damaged to recover on your own, you'll be just like him."

"I know," Riley said.

"It's an addiction, Riley. An addiction that kills."

Riley's expression flattened. "I know," she said again, remembering what Virgil had told her about dependency and withdrawal and how he'd made the corruption his own.

"He tried to stop drinking it." Her mother's view dropped to the edge of the round table in front of her. "Refused it after Patrick died."

Riley nodded.

"You know I was worried when you first started hanging around with him. Furious, in fact. I went over there to scream at Sam. Told her to keep him the hell away from you." She wiped one finger under her eye. "She said he didn't know anything about what he was. That he showed no signs, and she would never tell him. That's why she moved all the way out there. It was the farthest she could go while still receiving support for Pat's . . . service. So that she wouldn't have to work and could keep an eye on him."

She wiped at her face again.

"And when I saw you two, the way you seemed

so comfortable together, it was like seeing your father and Pat all over again." She looked up as a tear fell down her cheek. "They even laughed through their arguments." She sniffled. "I was worried when you wouldn't stop wearing his jacket that you would never move on. Every day it was just school, practice, and home. Nothing else. It seemed like Nate was the only one who could pull you out of that." She shook her head. "How could we stop you? Sam and I. How could we tell our children to not be friends without . . . " Her eyes closed. " . . . without telling them why?"

"You knew the whole time."

Her mother returned eye contact at last. "Of course, I did, dear. I spent half my life alongside *Father Pius*. I know every single one of their kind. Or I did. Haven't seen the records since . . . you know."

"Why didn't you tell me?"

"Why would I tell you? How would I tell you?" Her mother gestured as though not knowing how to answer. "'Oh, sweetie, you know your best friend, the one you hang out with all the time? Yeah, he's a werewolf, and your father used to drink his father's blood. Okay, you two go have fun now.'"

Riley clenched her jaw and shook her head.

"Why didn't *you* tell *me*?"

Riley didn't reply.

Her mother sighed. "Did you even *think* of talking to me before?"

"Before?"

"Taking the sacrament. Did you even think of asking me about it?"

Riley's shoulders sank. Her eyes dropped to the three casts she didn't need on her leg.

"That's what I thought."

Riley's mother stuffed the last of the clothes into the gaps in the box. She closed the top before disappearing behind the wall dividing the living room from her bedroom.

Riley pulled at the Velcro straps. They could all live openly now. They just couldn't live together.

She glanced up at the screen, a different camera captured footage of the brown and black wolf bounding over the barricades and across the trash left in the park. Two shots were fired by the police officers on screen. No way to tell if they hit.

The dropped-camera footage started again, the foot, the long nails. Riley turned on the sound and blinked quickly as the fangs appeared on-screen. Shadows disappeared around her as darkness covered her eyes.

She concentrated on the snarled sounds. "Leave us alone," she heard in the rumbled tones. "Please."

She gasped. This wasn't a threat. This was a plea.

She blinked out of the shadows and muted the TV when she heard her mother return.

"I'm leaving tomorrow," her mother said as she dropped another load of clothes on the table, "whether you come or not."

"I can't. I need to talk to him."

Her mother folded the clothes before putting them in a new box.

"Maybe I can work with him, like Dad did with his dad."

Her mother shook out a shirt before folding it.

"I know him," Riley said. "I can talk to him."

Her mother folded another shirt. "Sounds like you've decided," she said without looking. "Sounds like you decided a long time ago."

The video played again. Riley kept the sound off. She had heard all she needed.

"Leave us alone. Please."

# CHAPTER 10

FLEEING DRIVERS KNOCKED SEVERAL OF THE orange cones that separated the westbound lane to Juneau from the eastbound to Stumpvale. It took nearly an hour to get out of town using the one open lane that led past Nate's house.

Nate's mom stepped out before Riley could close her door. Riley walked around the car and stopped. She didn't need the crutches anymore, not even as a cover. Mrs. Wallace remained on the single step separating the entrance from the driveway, eyeing Riley up and down for a long moment. Heavy bags hung under Mrs. Wallace's eyes.

Riley looked toward the traffic to see if anyone was paying attention to the two of them out in the open. A pair of police officers who'd stopped Riley as she started to turn out of traffic waved the cars forward. Riley put her palms out to confirm that she was unarmed. She'd made a point of wearing short sleeves just for this reassurance.

Mrs. Wallace continued to inspect her. Her hair was grayer than Riley remembered from the last time she'd seen Nate's mom, two months ago during their Jack Nicholson movie night. Mrs. Wallace pursed her lips as though attempting to smile and motioned Riley forward.

She walked slowly as Mrs. Wallace fell in step behind her. Riley listened for the door to close. The house was exactly as she'd remembered from the hundreds of time she'd been there over the last ten years. Everything was the same and yet completely different. She was an invader now, stepping into enemy territory.

"Let me see," Mrs. Wallace said as she stepped

past and motioned for Riley to come into the kitchen filled with overhead light. Riley stepped forward, allowing Mrs. Wallace—a wolf, like her son—to tilt her face up and to the side.

"Much better than I imagined," she said.

Riley gave a quizzical look.

"The night you were brought in," Mrs. Wallace clarified as she stepped away, "it didn't look like the result would be so . . . subtle." She gestured for Riley to turn once more. "Yeah," Mrs. Wallace said, leaning in for a closer look. "Not too deep and not all . . . veiny." She stepped back once more. "You probably think they look hideous."

Riley had a slight tinge of shame as she nodded.

"You're young. One day they'll blend right in with the rest." Mrs. Wallace's eyes drifted away from Riley's. "Though I guess any new scars will only be on the inside."

Riley swallowed. "That's what they say."

"I'm glad you recovered," Mrs. Wallace said, glancing to Riley and then away. "If my people's blood has to go somewhere, well, better it go to you than anyone less . . . " She seemed to struggle finding the word. " . . . worthy."

"Thanks."

"How's your mom doing with all this?"

"She's not talking to me since I told her I wasn't leaving."

"Hmph. I know the feeling." Mrs. Wallace walked around toward the refrigerator. "You want anything to drink?"

"No thanks."

"You should. Leave, I mean."

"You know I can't."

Mrs. Wallace nodded, crossing her arms. "Well," she said with a sigh, "he's upstairs. Maybe he'll talk to you. Seems he always . . . " She shook her head and motioned for Riley to go.

"Thank you, Mrs. Wallace."

"Samantha," Nate's mom said. "Although, you'll probably never have occasion to call me that."

Riley made sure to step heavily and slowly on

each stair as she climbed toward Nate's apartment. She took the time to look over the pictures lining the staircase, of Nate's mother as a younger woman with light brown hair and a pretty, feline-esque face that she'd kept mostly intact, and of his father, the man neither of them ever knew, with deep-set eyes and a smile that shone through his dark beard. Hard to tell which parent Nate looked like more. Probably his mom's hair, maybe his dad's features, although it was difficult to know what was behind the beard. Riley didn't peek between the rails of the banister. She waited until reaching the exact top of the stairs—and the picture of baby Nate flanked by his parents—before turning.

He was seated on one side of the couch of his entertainment area, slouched with his elbows on his knees, facing the floor in front of the doorless entrance to his room.

"Hey," she said.

"Hey," he replied.

She walked toward him, heart pounding in her ears, trying to show no caution.

"Can I sit?"

"Free country," he said. "Kinda."

She sat. She placed one arm on the rest, the other across her body. It was too defensive. She put her hand on her leg instead.

He glanced over to her quickly before returning his gaze to the floor. "How does it feel?" he asked. "The leg I mean."

"Good. There's a big scar but other than that, healed up."

He nodded. "I've heard that's how it works."

"Yeah."

"And the scars on your face?"

She squeezed her eyes shut.

"Do they . . . hurt . . . at all?"

Her jaw clenched.

"I . . . umm—"

"I'd rather not talk about my scars," Riley interrupted.

Nate nodded. "I understand," he said. "Sorry."

Silence followed.

Her eyes scanned over the room, the large television on which they had watched probably hundreds of movies, the shelf of DVDs, all but maybe three of which she had seen, and the pair of doorways, one open and one closed. His sheets had been thrown onto the floor and the chair knocked over. Then there he was, still slumped over on the other side of the couch, short brown hair, a straight nose that turned up slightly at the bottom, and a narrow chin with a little bit of late-teen stubble starting to show.

"Hell of a way to make your television debut," she said.

"Which one?"

"Well, the restaurant was more of a teaser. Yesterday was the feature."

The corner of his mouth ticked up. His eyes closed as she nodded lightly. "I guess so." He glanced over to her. "Didn't know that no one would be able to understand what I said."

"I understood," Riley replied, turning away.

"Really?"

"Yeah, it's a senses thing." She couldn't get herself to face him. "An enhancement we get from, you know." She rubbed her hands together.

"If I'd known only you would understand then I would've said something cooler."

"'You can't handle the truth?'" she replied.

He seemed to chuckle a little. "I guess neither of us can."

After a moment, she said, "I had no idea about you."

"Neither did I."

"And I didn't even know about myself."

"I didn't know about you either," he replied. "Until yesterday."

"Same," she said.

"Hell, I didn't even know what I looked like or sounded like until it was shown to the whole world. Not in detail I mean. It's . . . "

She glanced over to see his eyes closed as though keeping in tears.

"I can see why they're scared." He covered his head with his hands. "I'm scared."

"Me too," she said, recalling how she jumped from the fangs appearing on her screen before the snarls and growls which she later decoded. "You said *please*," she continued a moment later.

"Yeah."

"'Leave us alone, please.'"

"Yeah," he said, glancing over to her.

"Does that mean me, too?" she asked.

Nate's eyes squeezed shut. His lip trembled.

"Maybe we could work together," she said.

"Not anymore." He shook his head as though in pain. "You're one of them. One of the people who attack and threaten us."

"Only because you attacked us first. That girl on the tracks. Her boyfriend."

"That wasn't us!" Nate's eyes were red as she

spoke. "That was your people trying to frame us. Frame me."

"What about in the woods three nights ago? Did you know one of your people killed one of mine?"

"That was defense, only after we were provoked."

"That's not what we do," Riley replied. "We're guardians."

"How do you know?" He twisted in his seat to face her.

"Because I've seen it," she said, turning to push her back into the armrest on the other side of the couch. "I saw it with my father. I saw it with Father Vigilius. He saved me the night of the accident. He pulled me from the wreckage."

"I did that!" he yelled. "I—" He stopped suddenly.

"What?"

His whole face seemed to turn down. He looked away, hiding behind his shoulder.

"What?" she said again forcefully.

"I was there," he said. "They chased me,

Virgil and Dove. Attacked me and made me turn into . . . what I am." She could hear his sobs as his back remained toward her. "I thought they would kill me, but then they stopped when you and . . . when you drove toward us."

Riley's head shook. She felt a sting in the side of her face, an ache in the back of her leg.

"Virgil shot out the tire," he said.

She remembered gravity shifting around her, pushing and pulling and tossing all at once.

"The scars on your face." He waved a finger vaguely at his right temple. "I did that. I didn't mean to." He looked down at his hand. "I just didn't know how sharp they were."

She remembered the light scratches that stung across her arms and face. She'd noticed them over the crushing pain in her leg.

"I pulled you out," he said.

She shook her head. It felt as though gravity were shifting again, pushing and pulling and tossing inside of her.

"I carried you to the hospital."

"You . . . started all of this? You?"

"They chased me!" he said again, turning toward her. His entire face was bright red, like the glowing eyes she'd seen in the wolf that towered over her.

"Why didn't you tell me any of this before?"

Nate said nothing.

"You could have told me any time you wanted. But you didn't. You could have told me everything and maybe none of this . . . " she waved her arm in the direction of the cars crammed on the road outside, " . . .none of it would have happened. But you didn't."

He still said nothing. He sat there, staring at her with his jaw locked.

"Remy died," she said, "and I almost died too."

"They followed me." His face was red and puffy, as though about to explode. She wondered if that was how their change started. "They used you to get to me."

"They'd been watching me. Virgil promised to keep me safe."

"Virgil's a liar!" His eyes flared and jaw snapped as he screamed.

"And you're a corruption!" she replied.

He stared at her, his face red and shaking. His eyes seemed to glow from within his skull. She fought the urge to jump from her seat.

He pulled back and turned away from her. He sat straight up, again looking at the floor in front of him.

"I know," he said. "And I'm tired of having to hide that because of . . . people like you."

"There wouldn't be any people like me if not for people like you." She felt the venom in her words.

"I thought you were my friend," he said.

"I thought you were human," she replied.

"I am."

She shook her head. "I came here because I thought that maybe we could work together, like our dads did."

"Your people killed my dad."

"He probably did something to deserve it."

He reeled from that remark. She regretted it immediately but tried not to show it. She couldn't seem weak in front of one of them.

"Get out," he said. "Leave us alone."

"Fine," she said. "If you leave *us* alone."

"Our town," he said.

"Our world." She turned toward the stairs. She didn't look back as she started her descent. "I hope I never see you again."

# CHAPTER 11

A FEW VEHICLES STILL PASSED ON THE ROAD, boxes stacked in the bed of trucks or the backseats and roofs of cars. Occasionally, drivers or passengers would stare at her, sitting alone on the bench in front of her apartment building, but soon refocused on getting out of the town as soon as possible. Probably thought she was one of them. That's the only reason anyone would stay. One of them.

Riley saw her mother in every car that passed. Riley was sure her mother was crying now, maybe even pulled off the road. Nothing she could do about that. Her path was chosen, long ago. No way to change it now.

A candy wrapper blew across the street in front of her. The stores and shops were dark, apartment windows and building entrances as well. The street-lights were starting to come up. Twilight in a ghost town. She looked over to the corner across from her building, the bank with the trash can chained to the lamppost. That was where she first noticed Virgil, a homeless man holding a piece of trash between the fingers of his surprisingly well-kept gloves and lick-ing whatever crumbs remained. She remembered the comments she and . . . he . . . had made, how ignorant they were. Ignorant about Virgil, ignorant about each other, themselves, everything. She'd been such a fool.

She looked up from the empty street, the softly glowing lamps above, to the last line of light riding the mountaintops raising up from the valley. The trees lit up all red and yellow and orange like a forest fire. A light haze hung in the air like smoke.

She looked down again. A flier on the lamppost on the sidewalk advertised a back to school sale at Fleet Foot Shoes on Tanacross Avenue, the big bridge road.

Riley pushed up from her side of the bench, the side she always sat on. The other was still his. She could have sat on that side if she wanted. She could have sat in the middle, taken up the entire seat. She didn't. Didn't even cross her mind until standing. It felt wrong to even touch it. She pulled up the hood of her jacket, it covered the top of her vision. It was time to leave.

This land belonged to *them* for now.

"I know there are some among you who may not agree with this new direction, but I assure you, by all that is holy, this change is not of our own doing, but the demand of our sacred mission. Each of you sacrifices your own humanity to protect that of others.

I say to you, today, at the dawn of this new world, let not your courage wane nor your faith falter. This is our time, the time we and generations before us have been preparing for. This is the time of our greatest blessing for we—*we*—have the honor of cleansing this world once more."

Father Vigilius followed his hand from the domed ceiling to the stone floor.

"The Earth will be pure again. The way the Lord intended."

He looked to the faces surrounding him. Those closest were worn and weathered, determined. Hardened warriors. Those stretching away, lining the walls and pushing together through the entrance, were fresh and new. Lambs and babes. They would learn or die, and do so quickly.

"We who are chosen. This"—he shook his hand for emphasis—"this cleansing is ours. It is our obligation, our burden, and our privilege. Our actions here will forever alter the fate of this world."

He spun quickly to look over them all. Darkness

covered their eyes. He shined to them, gleaming white under the candles overhead. This was the time he'd been waiting for, the time he'd been planning for. They'd look to him for guidance, and he would radiate such brilliance that they would never be lost again. It started here. He needed to show them the way.

He raised his open palms. "Our deeds will resonate throughout the heavens." His eyes followed his hands downward.

"Our names will be the books of a new scripture. One written without fear or darkness."

He clutched his fist as though snatching the air.

"We will reclaim this world for the one true God."

He paused, raised his chin.

"Brothers and sisters, we are no longer the Hidden Blade."

He opened his hand, palm up, fingers straight.

"We are the Pointed Hand."

This was the start. The crusade would begin. As he always knew it would.

His day would come.